EDDIE
BULWER'S
GROUND

EDDIE BULWER'S GROUND
Otis Carney

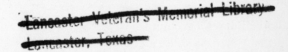

Walker and Company
New York

First published in the United States of America in 1987 by the Walker Publishing Company, Inc.

Published simultaneously in Canada by John Wiley & Sons Canada, Limited, Rexdale, Ontario.

Library of Congress Cataloging-in-Publication data

Carney, Otis.

    Eddie Bulwer's ground.

    I. Title.

PS3553.A757E3   1987   813'.54   86-32629

ISBN 0-8027-0953-2

Printed in the United States of America

10 9 8 7 6 5 4 3 2 1

To my own boys, and the old ones and the young ones who have worked our ground. Though all of us are just borrowing it for our time here, the hoofprints they lay on it and the sweat makes it more theirs than mine.

OTIS CARNEY
Cora, Wyoming
1986

EDDIE
BULWER'S
GROUND

CHAPTER 1

FOR a poor man, Eddie Bulwer had an empire. It was a piece of country maybe 20,000 acres in size that lay between the Beaver River in northwestern Wyoming and the tangled wilderness that sloped into Yellowstone Park. Of course, Eddie didn't own all this ground. It belonged to the people. Beaver National Forest. Eddie merely had an outfitting permit to let him guide hunters and fishermen here. All Eddie owned was one section where his ranch lay: 640 acres that had been homesteaded by Eddie's father and his Uncle Perce. And yet Eddie had, you might say, the keys to the kingdom. His father, old Yancey Bulwer, had figured out that due to the topography—a barrier of cliffs and blowdowns of lodgepole pine—this 640 acre valley was the only access to the vast basin that lay behind it. In 1889, when he homesteaded, Yance held the opinion that there'd never be a road up through here, and there still wasn't. You either came through the Bulwer ground to get into the basin, or you had to take the oil thirty-five miles west where, if it was dry, you might get in with a jeep on an old timber trail. But not very damn far. Yes, Eddie had that part of the Beaver sewed up. If you didn't go in with him, you had no business being there.

Eddie protected his territory like a cranky old grizzly bear. For several years now, he'd been convinced, or so he'd tell Doll, his wife, that they were going to take it away from him. "Who's they?" Doll would ask.

"The Forest Service and them," Eddie would grunt. Like most old-timers in the mountains of Wyoming, Eddie always

1

lumped some government body in with any potential assailant. But, the land grab never happened. If the truth be known, no other outfitter really wanted Eddie's section of country. With the blowdowns and bogs back there, you had to be about half mountain goat to get around. The average city hunter who answered an ad in *Field and Stream* just wouldn't fight country like that.

In addition, from the standpoint of the summer fishing trade, Eddie's area was pretty dry. Moon Creek wandered down the valley, but it only had small brook trout in it. Then, far back up against sheer cliffs called the Spines, there was one lake called Grubbing Hoe, after the shape of it. The cutthroat fishing was pretty good in Grubbing Hoe, at least so people had heard, but not many got in there for it because it was a helluva long pack and simply one small piece of water when you finally got there.

By comparison, any other comparable section of country in the Beaver drainage would have had three or four streams and maybe twenty lakes. So Eddie just kept his domain, whacked packhorses through it, and worshipped the big open silence and the freedom. Eddie Bulwer grew into his early sixties, still tough as a pine nut but a little tired now, and sour of disposition. Then, in August, the skies fell on him, and the world came in.

Eddie had finished haying the small meadow at the ranch August 20th; next morning, leading a packhorse, he started off up Moon Creek into the basin. Eddie had taken a big party from Denver into Grubbing Hoe Lake over the 4th of July. When he'd brought them back out, instead of striking his camp, he'd left it there, tents and cooking gear, figuring on getting more customers. But when nobody else came and other problems developed, Eddie never did go back for the camp. Now he knew he had to. In this part of Wyoming, you got ready for winter in late August; in fact, some years the Old Man would let down a snow shower during haying just to keep you plumb realistic.

But riding through the basin that day, you wouldn't have thought winter was anywhere close. In the black beaver ponds of Moon Creek, brookies were slapping up at mosquitoes, shimmering spray in the brilliant sun. The deerflies were out too, and, in the noonday heat, Eddie's horse was sweating and twitching flies as he started up the sliderock trail that led into the Spines and dropped down to Grubbing Hoe.

Up on this trail above timberline, Eddie could see about half the world, it seemed. Far below, in the tawny hay meadows of the big ranches, wound the silver snake of the Beaver River. Closer, the sagebrush hills lifted into lacy green aspen; Eddie could see faint dots of cattle here, summer ranges. Then the ground steepened and folded in over the high valley that was his ranch; the lodgepole forests raised like sentries, and thrusting up through them were fists of granite. From this distance, the old log buildings Yance Bulwer had built looked very small; between them and where Eddie rode was a sweep of dark timber, crinkled into valleys, then slashed open in parks and alpine meadows; here and there a massive lodgepole scorched by lightning and the dark earth below mouldering other tree carcasses that lay on the bones and skulls of buffalo. It was a virgin land yet, with a long memory.

On the sliderock trail, Eddie reined in, crooked his leg up over his saddlehorn, and rolled a cigarette. Then his eyes rested on this piece of the world he knew so well. There was a dark shadow at the edge of the trail below; not fully revealed, but Eddie saw it was a young bull elk. There'd likely be cows close behind him. Turning the other direction, to the rusty cliffs of the Spines, Eddie studied a place that looked like a cave but was actually a ledge. With the naked eye at perhaps a range of two miles, Eddie could see several little clumps that didn't belong. Or they did, yes. It was home to them: a band of mountain sheep. Higher still, over the vastness, two eagles coasted lazily on the shimmering waves of heat; and below Eddie in the slide rock, ground squirrels peeped out, wiggled their noses, and chirped at him.

Then, a sound began, as if from a trembling in the rock. It seemed to come up over the edge of the world and lay a streak of growl across the copper sky. Eddie turned toward the sound; his eyes were naturally squinted in the sunburned leather of his face, now they tightened as he watched a smoky feather tickle its way across the sky. Contrail of a jet.

Susan? Eddie whispered.

Then he could imagine his daughter Susan pointing down through the window of the jet, showing the people on board her home. Or maybe she'd be flying with the captain . . . what was his name, Price, Peters? Eddie had forgotten by now. Didn't matter. Captain Something from an airline— Eddie had taken him elk hunting five years before, got him a pretty good bull near Sawmill Park. Susan, fresh out of high school, had been camp cook. Sitting around the tent one night after hunting, the captain had said to Susan: Did you ever fly in a jet? When she said no, he said: Well, sometime while I'm still based in Salt Lake, you come down, and I'll take you on a trip.

Where do you go to? Susan asked.

The captain smiled. East to New York and west to Honolulu. That far enough?

Susan said, Pop, would you let me go?

Eddie said, sure, sometime, honey.

She did go, went to the training school of the line, got to be a stewardess in a sky-blue dress, and never came back.

"Aw hell," Eddie said aloud. "It ain't her flight. They don't get over this way."

He made a click with his mouth, swung his leg back off the saddle horn. The horse, Lester, began shuffling again up the sliderock trail, followed by a packhorse. Eddie reached the Spines, dismounted, and walked around through the wind-carved chimney rocks that studded the crest. About a thousand feet beneath him lay his one lake, Grubbing Hoe, emerald on a pillow of green meadow. Up from it came a raucous cry like the shriek of a bird: Eddie looked for a hawk. But now there was a shrill scream similar to a bobcat's, and then, clattering off the giant rock face, a gaggle of human sounds came echoing off the crystal face of the water and breaking it like sheet ice. Eddie gasped. There were bodies leaping, splashing into the milky mouth of the lake, and more running in from the meadow to join them. Male, female, their white skins were glistening in the sun, nothing to hide their private parts: they were buckass naked and squealing like pigs.

"I'll be damned!" Eddie cried. "Why, them . . . willya look at 'em!"

Who was he telling look? Lester, his horse? Or was it just a cry to the Old Man someplace: how dare they come in here! For even at this distance, Eddie could see that they were kids, dopeheads out of some city, dirty long-hair sons-of-bitches. They'd discovered the Shoshone Mountains way back in the hippie years and had been trooping back in tribes ever since. Eddie had heard the other outfitters and the Forest Service complaining because the trashy buggers were crawling all over the mountains like field mice. And now, apparently, they'd overrun the big forest, eaten it out until somehow they'd come way back here.

Muttering, Eddie mounted Lester and jerked the packhorse along the trail toward the lake; when he hit level ground, he struck the horses into a trot, their hooves clacking and showering sparks on the granite. He rode straight up toward the willow thickets where his tents stood on a ridge. Here, something howled. Eddie popped erect in his stirrups. There were two naked babies squalling in the grass and a third one sucking its mother's breast. The mother looked like a wild woman of Borneo, frizzy black hair, enormous haunches on her; she was big enough to eat hay.

By now, Eddie was trying to see nothing and see it all. There were campfires in front of the tents, and littered everywhere were empty cans and dry-food envelopes drifting in the wind. A wire had been strung between the trees, and there was meat and a few fish hanging. A guitar lay propped against a pine, and a heap of dirty laundry was piled on a rock beside the lake. It might have been all right if Eddie could have just kept looking at the things, but then the people came into it. They'd seen him by now. Some came blinking out of tents; they were dressed in animal hides, old black sweaters, headbands, army boots; one was playing a silly little flute. Then the bathers, they came too, striding up out of the water, the lead man wiping himself with an old brown towel; and the women, four, five, six of them: young girls, Susan's age. Them hoors! Eddie thought. Don't they show no shame! Up they came, switching through the tall grass, their wet hair hanging on them like drowned puppies. One made a giggling try at covering her parts with her hands but soon gave it up. Eddie pulled his eyes away from the spectacle of it. He sat there looking at his hands knotted on the saddlehorn, hoping the hoors would have the decency to go clothe themselves.

But the whole gang of them had soft voices, and they were purring at him, saying things like, "Hey, man, where did you come from?"

Finally, slowly, Eddie looked up. The women had sort of drifted away into the tents, and the nursing baby was now being packed on its mother's back. A few of the women returned wrapped in blankets. There were maybe twenty in the tribe, and most were standing around Eddie. They had these little grins on their faces, the one still playing the flute and another rotating his palm up beside his eyes like he was washing a window, and saying, "Hi. Hi . . ."

"How long," Eddie said hoarsely and to nobody, "have you been here?"

"Just passing the time," somebody said. Obviously nobody in this bunch would have a calendar. They kept grinning at

Eddie. Finally a big fellow with a red beard scowled at the others.

"Don't rip the man off," he said. "The man asked a nice question. Have we been here long? Well, like two, three weeks. If it matters."

"It does to me. This is my permit, private property you're using."

"Oh but it's not," piped a pointy-nosed girl with thick eyeglasses. "We have a map. This is national forest. The ranger showed us just where to go."

"Well he damn well didn't show you to camp in my tents, use my gear!"

Redbeard moved next to Eddie's horse. "Now cool it, man. In the first place, we came upon this . . . windfall, this joint in the wilderness. There was no sign. Nobody said, trespass thee not."

"How did you get in here?" Eddie muttered.

"Flew. We flew all the way from Schenectady."

"Yeah," said another of them "we just grooved on in—"

"Hey, come on," a girl said sternly to the one who'd spoken. Then, pinning her wet blonde hair on top of her head, she glanced up at Eddie. "We started at the ranger station and walked. Followed a trail on one of those red and white maps they give you."

"There ain't no marked trail that comes near this lake," Eddie said, "so how'd you find it?"

"Look man, are you the gestapo or something?" Now it was Redbeard again and backed by a lanky dark one with greasy bangs. "We walked off the road someplace back there . . . " Redbeard waved toward the west, "came to this camp, it was made for us. We don't bother anybody, they don't bother us. There hasn't been a single hassle until you came along."

Wearily, Eddie jerked Lester around and walked him over to a dead pine where he always tied up. Lester knew. He edged to the tree as Eddie tied his halter, then tied the packhorse and uncoiled the ropes from the pack saddle. Eddie stood for a moment with his hands on his hips, blew a long breath. Where to start? Everyplace he looked, he saw litter. The portable toilet seat Eddie had left at the camp in case some hunter or fisherman insisted on using it was now nailed to a tree with toilet paper festooned around it—and pine boughs cut and arranged like it was supposed to be some object of art.

Eddie shook his head, walked over to the tree and jerked down the toilet seat. It came off in a squeal of the nail which, Eddie now saw, had split the seat. He looked at it glumly: no more good: well, throw that away. Only Eddie didn't throw junk around in the woods like some of them; he dropped the toilet seat into the pannier on the packhorse: maybe Doll would glue it for him.

Then he walked over to the closest fire, in front of the tent where the babies were playing. His old gray coffee pot was on the fire, his biscuit sheet lying in the coals with a crimp in it like somebody had stepped on it. He also saw the grill he'd welded one winter, with hooks to hang dutch ovens on; but he could only find one hook, so he got down on his hands and knees and rummaged through the dirt to find the other one.

As he knelt there, he became conscious of several naked hairy legs near his face. One pair of legs wore black motor-cycle boots. "What're you doing, man?"

"Well, first, I'm trying to find what belongs to me," Eddie said slowly. Then he looked up: Redbeard and Greasy Bangs were standing above him, with others ringing behind. "There was hooks in here, five of 'em. I'll thank you to dig up what you been using of mine, set it over there by the packhorse so I'll see what I still got left. I'll strike the tents myself."

Taking the coffee pot and the biscuit sheet, Eddie stood up slowly. A pregnant girl, bulging out of a buckskin shirt, was standing in front of him. "The tents are our homes. He can't take the tents, can he?" She looked around at the rest of the tribe.

"I made some of them tents, Sissie," Eddie said wearily, "bought the rest of 'em. They belong to me. Now goddammit—"

He strode past her up to the first tent, jerked back the flap. A stink of something burned, probably drugs of some kind, stung in his nostrils; then there was perfume and grease and just plain body sweat. Inside the tent, he pulled at blankets, a kid's doll, beads, some books—Eddie couldn't see—he flung everything out the flap. When he backed out, dragging another blanket and a pair of cut-off Levis, the tribe had made another ring around him and just stood there watching him work.

Once he'd emptied the tents, he squatted down and began to pull out the ground pegs. But every place he'd try to move there'd be a knot of trashy buggers in the road. Eddie saw what they were doing, kind of a sitdown strike, it seemed.

"Believe I could be out of your way quicker if you'd give me a hand here," Eddie said. Nobody answered. Finally, Eddie butted through and started pulling up the end pegs. Then somebody tapped his shoulder. He whirled. It was Redbeard with Greasy Bangs next to him. "You're not taking the tents, gramps. They're our homes. You're not about to take them."

Eddie thrust up. He was six foot four, slow to anger, maybe wizened looking in the face, and getting old and somewhat bronc-crippled too; but in that instant, the slow-burned fuse burst into a red ball of blood that blinded him. "You sons-of-bitches!" Eddie cried. "You don't tell me what I can do! Now get in here and help me clean this camp— what you done to it—or I'll whip the goddam lot of you!"

Somebody laughed: "Oh, will you now?"

Greasy Bangs was snickering at Eddie and Redbeard patting him on the shoulder. They were the closest objects Eddie saw: targets: fire! He felt Greasy Bang's cheek rising

under his fist; that was his left, and his right catapulted into
the belly of Redbeard, the beard falling next to Eddie's face
and the mouth spitting a gassy cry. Then it was arms and
legs, the whole roaring tribe leaping on, Eddie kicking and
fighting as more piled on top of him. He kept thinking about
going to get his axe: his good axe was strapped on his saddle.
But they had him down now, some holding his arms, others
kneeing into his stomach. One was wrapping a tent rope
around his legs. They were howling, screaming; Eddie tasted
blood in his mouth. Then, in a bearlike lurch, he thrust up,
slashing the arms and faces that were holding him down. For
just an instant, he staggered up free in the sun. The women
were screaming, and he saw Redbeard down on all fours like
a dog and puking. Then there was a swish in the air, an
object whirling close to Eddie's ear. His head reverberated
in the throb of a monstrous gong; he was blind, the grass
pulling him down, the black inside of a tent collapsing over
him and taking the world away.

Eddie moved slowly and painfully out to the porch of the
log house. It was suppertime now, the sun slanting down and
aching his eyes. On the porch, Eddie had his gunrack and,
beneath it, a cabinet he'd carpentered where he kept shells
and reloading equipment. When he bent down to open the
cabinet, the top of his head like to come off; in the pain, he
clenched his teeth, and now they were aching too from the
gnashing. But he managed to reach into the cabinet and pull
out a box of 30.06 ammunition; then, for a moment, he
balanced the red and green Winchester box in his palm:
jacketed bullets, they'd kill. He thought better of it. He
leaned again in pain into the cabinet and pulled out a dusty
box of shotgun shells that he'd reloaded. Then, he raised up
toward the Remington pump, which was roughly equivalent
to a riot gun. He'd used one like it in the Marine Corps for
herding Jap prisoners. It'd work just right now. He lifted it
off the deer's-feet rack.

As he turned, his wife, Doll, was standing in the porch doorway, leading into the house. She was wearing carpet slippers and a blue flowery dress. Her hands were on her hips and her high, Hungarian cheekbones glinted in the sun; she looked about half like she was laughing, but all she said was, "My my. This is going to be a real smart thing to do."

Eddie motioned for her to go in the house; her hand reached out for him, then her long fingers trailed up the back of his head and touched his scalp. "Eddie?"

He pulled away, walked past her into the kitchen, and set down the Remington and the shell box. There Doll caught him, and her green eyes snapped. "Go to the telephone, Eddie. Talk to Ly . . . he's on . . . "

Ly—Dr. Lyman Bulwer—was their son, dentist, living over in Laramie. "Well by damn," Eddie grunted, "my teeth are hurting bad enough to talk to him."

"Listen, Pop," Ly said when Eddie picked up. Doll had called him. "You can get yourself into something serious here. You got mom worried. You can't take the law into your own hands. Sure, they're kooks, birds-and-bees people or whatever, but they've got just as much right to use that forest as you do."

"Don't tell me what I can and can't do! That's how them trashy buggers got started—"

"Pop," Ly pleaded, "press charges. Put in a call to the sheriff, he'll handle it for you. But if you go up there and shoot somebody . . . "

"If I do," Eddie said, "it'll be somebody who needs it."

And so they wrangled on for a moment or two more until Doll took the phone away. "They've hurt him," Doll said to her son, "made him awful mad. And, you can't tell him anything, not when he gets to bulling like this." Then she laughed and said, "Maybe, Ly, you can work on his teeth in the prison, when you make your rounds over there."

"Ask him what the hell to take for my teeth." Eddie growled. Then, reminded of the pain again, he stalked into the pilot in the butane furnace. On the log walls were elk, moose, deer heads that Eddie had taxidermed himself; learned it by correspondence course, passed one winter that way, then got tired of it and went on to looking at TV. Blowing out a long breath, Eddie sagged down in his big chair by the fireplace. He leaned forward, dropped his head into his hands. The damned ache; they'd whopped him with a frying pan on top of the skull, knocked him clean cold; when he came to, they'd hauled him and his horses a couple of miles down the trail and left him. After Eddie had felt around at his aches and realized he wasn't hurt all that bad, his temper burst on him again; he'd snatched the axe off his saddle and began to run back up the trail; well, he ran a few yards anyhow until that knot on his head throbbed and the revenge just drained out him. But he'd sure come back for the buggers and come right this time. That was what carried him home, gnashing his teeth—"a bad biblical habit"—Ly jokingly had told him. But Eddie'd had a jaw injury in the war; Ly wouldn't understand something like that. He just thought it was Eddie's nerves or his constant mad against the world that made him gnash.

Then Eddie scrunched his eyes closed, and, for a moment, he thought of Junie, comparing him to Ly. Junie was their oldest kid; he was the one who used to hunt with Eddie, help him taxiderm; Junie was a rough old boy; some people said he was dumb as a post, but that wasn't true. Junie had had some trouble at birth, and he hadn't developed as fast maybe, not as quick as Ly. But Junie was strong and filled with sheer blundering guts. Hell, he would have walked back up that mountain trail today and pounded them dopers' heads in the sliderock. Yessir, Junie, Eddie chuckled inwardly, if while they was holding me down, you could have slid out that axe, then for damn sure we would have christianized 'em.

Doll came into the parlor. She cocked her head. "They got you so ringy you're talking to yourself now?"

Eddie shook his head and scrunched his eyes closed again. "You talking to Junie?"

Eddie nodded.

Then he heard Doll's dress crinkle. She sat on the arm of his chair; her face came next to his, the smell of perfume faint and with it that carbolicky clean smell she got from the clinic where she was a nurse. Doll's shoulders gave a kind of shudder, then Eddie felt the warm wet of her tears on his cheeks. For who? Junie? Lying dead in a jungle in Vietnam, never even found; or for old Eddie, fighting on now alone? Thirteen years Junie had been gone, but they, neither of them, were over it yet. Every day, something would remind Eddie of the boy.

Doll took a long sighing breath and dabbed at her nose. "Ly says he's calling a prescription to town for you. Help your teeth. And I'm going to put an ice pack on your head. That's the best thing."

"It ain't gonna fit under my hat," Eddie said. "Now move . . . " He lifted her gently. "I'm going back up there."

She followed him out to the kitchen without saying a word. Methodically, he slipped on his hunting coat, began filling the pockets with shells. Then he racked the slide of the pumpgun back and forth several times, being sure it was empty and also not jamming. "I got some dinner for you," Doll murmured. "You ought to eat at least before you go."

He shook his head. "Be dark now when I get there."

"That's right. So why go? What can you do in the dark?"

"Because . . . ," Eddie blurted, but couldn't say anything more.

She gripped him with her strong wiry arms behind his shoulders. Again, her fingers trailed up to the top of his scalp, the aching lump. "You'd always go, wouldn't you? You got to fight your way. Eddie, can't you see it's different? It isn't guns and fights anymore. Just look at today, those kids. Look what they did to you."

"And you'd let 'em off, I suppose. Say they was sick, get your doctor friend to treat 'em?"

"Eddie . . . they just show you . . . if you weren't so stubborn you'd realize it . . . they show you how much things have changed around here. It isn't your private country anymore, that permit, this ranch, none of it. You can't put up a fence and keep out the city trash or the cabin sites or the coke plant—crime, drugs, whatever. All those things you hate, Eddie, are coming in here. Don't you think I see 'em at the clinic? And you, you poor old hoss, you're back in the mountains so much, you're away from it, you don't know what's happened to the rest of the world. And you don't want to. There," she whispered, "doesn't that feel better?"

She had him sitting now on the kitchen table and had slid the ice pack up onto the knob. Hell, he didn't know if it felt better or worse, but somehow in the way she was gripping him and caring about him . . . she seemed the one thing left in the world that August night that hadn't done a somersault. So Eddie just sat there with his arm around old Doll's hips. Soon he got the idea he'd have a good jolt of whiskey. They each had a couple, in fact; and the Remington pump was still on the table when she took him off to bed.

The town of Beaver, Wyoming, lay in the foothills of the Shoshone Mountains. It had one paved main street, nine hundred-plus people, the courthouse, jail, undertaker, five saloons, eight motels, one medical clinic, three churches, the Wyoming Game and Fish office, the U.S. Forest Service office, and a private telephone company with a new electronic switchboard designed to handle the calls for all of Beaver County, three thousand people in a land mass of five thousand square miles. But despite the modern equipment, the chances are if you had tried to make a call in Beaver or Beaver County between 9:35 a.m. and about noon on August 21, you would have gotten a busy signal or no answer. Everybody was either on the phone or out at the neighbors telling about what happened to Eddie Bulwer. It began when Eddie walked into the drugstore where he'd finally located Pankey Briles, the sheriff. Eddie said, "I got a matter for you, Pankey. You want me to wait over in your office?"

"Hell, set, Eddie," Pank said, grinning. He and one of the state troopers were sitting at the drugstore counter stirring their coffee. Pankey carried two guns on his hips; some said he liked to swagger around the drugstore in summer, particularly when there were so many pretty tourists in little sunbathing costumes. Or maybe he spent so much time at the drugstore for sentimental reasons: Pankey had once been a soda tosser there before he took on politics. Anyhow, Pank said to Mabel Doane behind the counter: "Give Eddie some coffee."

"On you or the county?" Mabel wisecracked.

"Hell, I don't want none," Eddie grunted. "Look, Pank, I'll make this quick. I been in a scrap. I want you to go after some people or I'm going myself and shoot the sons-of-bitches."

Eddie had said this very quietly between clenched teeth; but Jack Wasson, who was a 47-year-old box boy at the grocery store, coffeeing two seats down the counter, he heard it; and Mabel Doane lifted her eyes above her glasses and squinted at Eddie. Now, there was a few b.s. artists around town you could accuse of starting a story just to bring attention to themselves. And there was the kind who couldn't pick up the truth if it was a dollar bill on the sidewalk—had to exaggerate everything and were always hanging around the motels or the saloons big mouthing to whoever'd listen. But when Eddie Bulwer came in from the back country with a couple of bruises on his face and limping a little . . . Eddie was a man who didn't want any part of town, and few people there knew him, except that he was an old timer and the Bulwers tended to their own.

Mabel quickly grabbed the coffee jug and started back down the counter to refill Pankey and the patrolman, though

Mabel quickly grabbed the coffee jug and started back down the counter to refill Pankey and the patrolman, though they were just filled a moment before. By the time she reached them, the patrolman was standing up digging in his pocket for change. "Let's get out of here, Pank, discuss this over at your place."

Mabel rushed to the phone and Jack Wasson to the grocery store. *Didja hear about Eddie Bulwer? Got into a fight with . . . who? Some poachers, killing elk to get the ivory teeth. No, drug pushers, part of a drug ring that's moving in on the county. Hell, it was the neighbors up there, the Galushas: They'd accused Eddie of stealing their calves.*

Like a jungle tom-tom, the story throbbed all over Beaver. By afternoon, however, the facts had been pretty well corrected in terms of assailants. Pankey's deputy's girlfriend had taken care of that during the lunch hour. That afternoon, people brooded along the boardwalk streets and out in the hay meadows. Stinking city longhairs beating up a man in his own camp. What was the country coming to? And into supper that night, around the saloons and the cook houses of ranches, folks had pretty much concluded that them animals that beat up Eddie Bulwer were really part of a bigger gang, you might say an army.

It had come to somebody's attention (nobody knew just which somebody) that California bike gangs and the earth people from somewhere had now decided to take over the state of Wyoming. After all, there were only 320,000 people in the state, 186,000 voters approximately. So with probably one hundred thousand love culters and dopers coming in, voting control of the state could be taken away from the honest people. All hell would break loose. A state for scum: drugs, fornication, with punk rock as the official anthem. And more than one leathered Beaver resident muttered, By God, if Eddie had shotgunned the whole bunch of 'em, there wouldn't be a man in the county—hell, in the state—that would try him for murder!

There was only one trouble with rumors in Beaver County. To get really ornate they needed time to grow: up in this isolated land, the natives were true artisans at liecraft. But in the case of Eddie Bulwer's story, it got shot down by midafternoon that same day. The damn Forest Service and them shot it down.

For once in his life, Pankey Briles had made a quick move. Well, really, the patrolman suggested it. Since the incident happened on national forest, why not get the government involved? They had the money and a helicopter to fly out in immediate pursuit. A half hour later, the regional ranger and a young district assistant—both armed—Pankey and the pilot set out for Eddie's camp at Grubbing Hoe Lake. Of course, Eddie was with them, but they didn't let him carry a gun. He was just there for identification purposes.

Two hours later, the helicopter had popped its way back to the Beaver airport and a glum little crew descended. "It ain't that I'm doubting you, Eddie," Pankey Briles was heard to say. "The evidence is sure there, the mess they made. But you know how it is now up in the forest. There's so many of these kids back there anyway, I don't know how we're ever going to find yours. They can just melt in among some of them camps or the backpacker outfits."

"Well, I can sure identify that redhead and the one with greasy bangs and a couple of them girls. Hell, there was one so remarkable ugly, she could go bear hunting with a switch."

"I would advise, Briles," said the district ranger, "that you start shaking down some cars leaving the forest area. For example, on that timber road west of Eddie's permit, we saw that VW bus. That could have carried some of them."

"Good idea," Pankey said; he'd sure attend to blocking off some roads and looking at faces.

"I suppose," volunteered the younger ranger, "that Eddie might draw a picture of the two he spoke about. We did that once up in Yellowstone."

Eddie grunted. "You ain't got no artist in me, brother. But show 'em to me, and I'll tell you which."

"Well," Pankey Briles said. They'd now all walked to the Forest Service jeep and the sheriff's car at the edge of the airport. "Well, I don't know what else we can do, Eddie. If we hunt somebody up, you can make a complaint after i.d. And, you aren't out any gear, are you?"

Eddie shrugged. "Won't know until I get back up there and count it."

Then the Forest Service and them said it was a crying shame the way these mountains were filling up with trash; and they hoped Eddie's head got better, etc. They'd be in touch with him if they picked anybody up. As they drove away, Eddie stood in the parking area beside his pickup, then gave a swipe with his boot, and gravel stung out against the side of his truck like buckshot on a trashy bugger's butt. Wearily, Eddie turned and started to get in the truck, go home, forget the whole damn thing.

But a man in a red shirt was walking around the end of the hangar. "Hey," he hollered, "Eddie."

It was Joline Roush, the head game warden. While Eddie and them were walking across the airport discussing the city creeps, Eddie had noticed the Game and Fish plane land, Joline flying it. Joline wasn't a bad old boy except he and Eddie were on different sides of the fence, you might say.

"Can you give me a ride to town?" Joline asked.

"Yas." Eddie opened the truck door for him, and Joline got in carrying a leather briefcase. Joline took off his big-brimmed hat and smoothed down his sleek black hair. Joline had hair that grew almost to his eyebrows; some of the poachers used to call him Ape, but outside of that irregularity, he was a pretty nice looking fellow, a few years younger than Eddie, had them red rosy cheeks that were probably Mormon in origin. But Joline as a warden was straight and tough, and Eddie had learned to give him plenty of distance.

"I just heard about your wingding at camp," Joline said.

"I've got a couple of boys checking fishing licenses in the forest. I'll have them keep their ears open. We might run onto something."

Eddie shook his head. "It ain't getting beat up that bothers me, Joline. It's by whom. But hell, Pankey and them, they'll never find nothing, couldn't find their ass with both hands. It don't matter, I suppose."

Joline nodded. Eddie offered him a cigarette, but of course Joline didn't smoke. Eddie lit up and cracked the truck window to blow away the smoke. Then he had to slow because the Mooneys were moving cattle; the Mooneys had some meadows near the airport and a few old black ballie cows. Mavis Mooney was out there horseback, clacking the cows off the oil road, while Jack, her old peg-legged husband, he was walking in the bar pit beside the road. Eddie rolled down the window. "You're either on a short horse, Jack," he said, "or you're a damn sheepherder."

"I figured you to be in the hospital," Jack said, referring of course to the fight.

Eddie chuckled; and by then he'd eased the truck through the cows and started to pick up speed again. He almost didn't hear Joline Roush when he said: "Eddie . . . I got a— *you* got a problem."

"Oh?"

At first Eddie thought Joline was building up to some joke or something about the trash. But Joline had opened his little briefcase and pulled out a file of papers. "I was in Cheyenne today, Eddie, meeting with the State Game Warden. He asked me to ask you about a couple of hunters, bear hunters you had, between the twenty-sixth of May and the first of June. Do you remember those hunters?"

Eddie frowned. Just the way Joline talked, that serious straight manner of looking at a lot of official papers in his lap . . . that made Eddie's neck bristle, and his face go hot. "Well yas," Eddie said. "Couple of fellows from Texas.

Royd, I believe one was called. Funny damn name, makes you remember it. The other was, what the hell . . . ?"

"Enfield. McMurray R."

"That's right. Called him Mac. They wasn't bad fellers. What about 'em?"

"Well, you tell me, Eddie. They got a bear, did they?"

"Yas. One brown. Two-year old, he was. Legal. Fished a little too. What's the matter, anyway?"

Joline leafed through the papers on his knees, and, by now, Eddie was hardly paying attention to the road. He could see the town of Beaver, the first motel signs beginning to rise up ahead out of the sagebrush.

"Eddie, on the afternoon of the twenty-eighth, until late that same night, did you leave the hunters back up in your permit, in the vicinity of Arapaho Sink?"

"Ah hell," Eddie said. "Twenty-eighth. I don't remember, Joline. Say! By God, yas, that was that afternoon I did take off. You know, the Sink ain't but about two hours ride from my house. Royd and old Mac there, they was pretty tired, wanting to quit hunting just for then, so I did leave 'em, Joline, you bet. I know it ain't recommended. But they ain't bad boys. They been in the woods before."

"I guess they have," Joline said. "By the way, what did you go out for, Eddie?"

Now Eddie slowed the truck; they were entering the outskirts of Beaver. His foot felt tired and heavy on the brake; and the brake pulled, needed new lining on the drums, another thirty or forty bucks. "Doll and I was figuring Susan—that's our girl—she was supposed to come home for her mother's birthday. I don't get to see Susan much now, lives over in California. So I just rode down, set around the house waiting. She never did come. Called though."

Joline nodded. "Eddie. Were you conscious of anything when you came back to the camp? Any change?"

Eddie frowned. "Hell, Joline, I don't know. Them boys had been drinking a little, as I remember." Eddie jammed the brake again harder: the Game and Fish log building was just off to the left down a dirt street. Eddie turned. "What are you getting at, Joline?" he said sharply. "You trying to put something in my mouth?"

"They already did, Eddie."

"Who?"

"Royd and this Mac Enfield. They drove out of here over Route 80 to eastern Wyoming. On the way, they stopped in a restaurant in Laramie. Coffee House. They were sitting in a booth talking pretty loud. Or loud enough so that Andy Betts, a warden down there, heard 'em. They'd picked up a girl in Laramie, and they were telling her how they had a bear hide out in the car, and they also had elk meat. She said, 'Out of somebody's freezer?' And one of them answered, no, they'd shot at the bear and hit an elk behind him . . . or something to that effect. Some smartalecky answer. Anyhow, while they were still in there talking, Andy Betts went and got a warrant. They searched the car and found an elk hind quarter, that's all, just one lousy hind quarter."

Eddie lurched the car to a stop in front of the Game and Fish building. The breath sagged out of him. He stared at his big thick dumb hands gripping the truck wheel. "Them sons-of-bitches," he whispered. "How'd they do it? Joline, I ain't lying to you! I never knew that!"

"We believe you, Eddie," Joline said. "But it doesn't matter anyway because they were under your control, on your permit."

"How did they do it?" Eddie cried.

Joline hitched his leg up against the dashboard and began to read. It was a sworn statement from Royd; how after Eddie'd left to go home afternoon of the twenty-eighth, they'd seen a young bull elk come out of the timber; watched him for quite awhile, finally couldn't resist. Shot him, then got scared about Eddie learning of it. So they dressed him out, keeping only one hind quarter and stashing that in an old beaver dam near camp. They buried the rest of the carcass in the soft bog of Arapaho Sink. The next day, pretending he needed some stomach medicine, Enfield split off from Eddie and Royd, took a pack horse and pannier down to the ranch. What he did was to take the hind quarter into town, where an old army buddy lived, put it out on his back porch where it was still cool enough to keep. Eddie never did know a thing about it. . . .

"But still," Eddie murmured, "my responsibility. My permit." He swung to Joline: "What are you going to do?"

"We have an exact spot where the carcass is supposed to be buried. Got to go up there, take you up—if it's there, Eddie . . . " Joline shook his head. "It could mean your permit."

"A fine, you're saying."

"Take your permit. Revoke it."

"God, Joline, that's my livelihood. I don't know how to do nothing else!"

"We're all sorry about it. Just a bad break, but dammit, you got to see the state's point of view too. We license certain outfitters to protect the law. Protect the game herds, you know that."

"Yas, yas. Hell, I spare and save more game than I ever shoot. I would have hacked those bastards, Royd and him, if I ever caught 'em."

"But you didn't, Eddie, that's the point. I'm not saying you've been casual in the past, but when you take a hunter out, it's not a good idea to leave him. Things like this happen. Now, when do you want to go in? Tomorrow morning?"

Eddie's eyes were scrunched closed. He just kept shaking his head. "I guess so," he muttered.

"See you at the ranch then," Joline said, slamming the door. "Thanks for the ride, Eddie."

Yeah, Eddie said inwardly. The ride of my life.

CHAPTER 2

THAT next morning was muggy and threatening to storm, no day to be digging in a bog, what with the deerflies and gnats. For a time, Eddie dug around with Joline and the boy warden who was helping him. Then Eddie went back up out of the bog to a spring to get a drink. He squatted there under the pines, looked out at the rumbling gathering clouds. Then he lit a cigarette. Joline and them were getting paid to find the evidence. It didn't mean nothing to Eddie but his career.

Well, Eddie thought, trouble always did come to this place. Old Arapaho Sink must have had a long history. It lay in a fairly steep valley that crooked around like a hog's leg; the valley floor here under the shadowing lodgepole looked like a meadow, but actually was a squashy yellow bog, smelling of sulphur and having one or two deep holes in it you could sink out of sight in. The way the bog lay, surrounded by thick forest and good springs, had made it a natural place for game to hide out. And a trap too. Eddie believed you could probably find dinosaurs down in that bog. He had once found a bone that didn't fit any animal he knew. And of course he'd plumbed up quite a few buffalo skulls out of the Sink. It appeared that the Indians were in the habit of shooting game back here; they probably drove a herd into the valley, got it bogged down, and thus they saved a lot of arrowheads. God knows, Eddie had found enough arrowheads and scraping tools, sprinkled in the blowdowns around the edge of the Sink.

It was Eddie's half brother Dwayne (Doc they called him)

who'd first taken Eddie up there, many damn years ago. Doc had been born in 1899, son of Yancey Bulwer's first wife; and, a year or two later, Cyril followed. When they were just toddlers, so Doc told Eddie, Shoshones, Arapahoes, Blackfeet—any of 'em who happened to be in the country—they'd usually hunt this Sink and then come trailing down the creek to the big meadow behind the Bulwer log cabins. Doc said he and Cyril would wake up some morning, and there'd be a hundred or so teepees, mongrel dogs snapping, and Indian ponies grazing everywhere. Then up toward the house would clump a delegation of bucks wrapped in blankets, carrying rifles of a pretty good make, like Winchester.

One time, Pappa Bulwer had gone to the chores, and Doc and Cyril were alone when the braves come pounding on the back door. The boys went headfirst down into the cellar, and Doc always carried a scar where he'd banged his forehead against the rock wall. When nobody answered the door, the Indians finally busted in. But they didn't take anything that time, just left Yancey some beadwork he was buying for his new bride, who turned out to be Eddie's mother.

Another time when Doc was young, the Sink had figured in an outlaw story too. A man named Krosik, reported to have killed a sheepherder over in Lander, had been trailed up to the Bulwer ranch. The sheriff wanted to go after Krosik himself because there was a five-thousand-dollar reward. However, the sheriff also didn't know his way around the Sink or Bulwer territory, so, in the late evening, he rode up to the cabin alone and asked Yance to guide him up to the Sink. Well, Eddie's mother was just a new bride at the time, but she loved old Yancey and had a pretty good head on her too. She sized up the sheriff, who wasn't any big imposing figure or marksman either. Then she said, Yes, Mr. Bulwer could go with the sheriff but under one condition: that they take along the oldest son, Doc, then eight years old.

The sheriff was puzzled and a little fearful of this request.

"Ma'am," he said, "we're going against a known killer who will probably shoot on sight; therefore I don't believe it's advisable to have a child with us."

"That's just exactly why I want him with you," Eddie's mother said. "Chances are you'll be shot dead first off, sheriff. And Mr. Bulwer might just be wounded. But no outlaw is going to kill an eight-year-old. So the boy will come back and tell me where your bodies are, and I can go fetch you."

Well, Doc went, and he told the story for many years. Just like Eddie's mother predicted, the sheriff did get shot, not bad, just in the shoulder; both Yance and Doc got away and managed later to haul the sheriff out by roping and tying him on his horse. Krosik made himself scarce and lived another six months before a man shot him dead in a saloon fight in Opal.

Despite the kind of letdown of it, old Doc did love telling that story, describing the full moon and the light snow, the crunch-crunch of their feet as they approached the dark Sink, knowing that desperado was crouching there waiting for them. And the sheriff booming out, just like on TV: "In the name of the law you're under arrest!" Karrow! Doc would roar and make a jerk like a gun going off. That would be Krosik spinning the sheriff down. "What did you do, Doc?" Eddie'd ask.

"Hell, bud, I just bellyflopped into that snow and rotten leaves and skedaddled like a lizard down into a little draw. Karroom, Karroom! More shooting. Finally, pappa come for me in the draw and said, 'We're gonna get out of here,' and we sure did."

Squatting there under the pines, with a black rain beginning to dapple down, Eddie could almost hear Doc again, and Cyril with him. It seemed so far back now, that those two were part of this world of Eddie's when it was a frontier; hell, Doc was twenty years older than Eddie, and Cyril eighteen. Growing up, Eddie worshipped them. But after

Eddie grew up, things rotted out with Doc. And Cyril—he went in the navy or merchant marine, and wrote letters for a few years until they plumb lost him. Eddie always expected Cyril to turn up; he was a kind of bad penny who just might, too.

By now, Eddie's cigarette was out, and Joline was squishing slowly toward him across the bog. Eddie got up, leaned his forearm up against a pine and waited. It was like a sentence from a judge, what Joline said; he pointed at the far end of the bog where the boy warden was dragging up a rusty brown carcass; the bog water had kept it in pretty good shape: remains of an elk, this summer's kill. Then there was a silvery flash. Eddie saw another youngster from the Game and Fish blinking a camera away as the warden dragged the carcass out of its hole.

"You ain't leaving nothing to the imagination," Eddie muttered.

Joline was sitting down, peeling off his waders. He shook the water out of them, then gave a little jerk, for there was a snap-crash of lightning close, leaving a burned smoky smell over the dark crooked Sink. "We got to pin it down, Eddie," Joline said quietly. "We're going to hack those two guys. It'll help everybody."

"I ain't too sure of that."

Joline stood up, the rain pattering now on his big tan hat. He moved in beside Eddie under the pine. "I'll be going back down to Cheyenne, Eddie, and I'm going to try to help you all I can. But it may not be much. The department, in fact the whole state, is coming under heat from the environmentalists. We had that big predator fight about killing coyotes and lions; then the eagle shooting business and that ring up in the Big Horns that was slaughtering elk and selling them. Well, the department has got to be absolutely as clean as a hound's tooth. If there are violators, regardless of whose friends they are . . . if the law has been broken, there's going to be punishment, spelled out by the book. Furthermore, we're going to publicize it, put the fear of God around. So that's the background. I'll go to bat for you as best I can."

Then Joline walked over to the edge of the Sink to help the others. Eddie just swung over Lester and stared at the carcass as they lashed it on the packhorse. "For that miserable thing," he muttered. Then the rain really dumped down, rattling, stinging. Eddie hollered that they should follow him; there was a trail he knew that'd be dry. It took off from a little draw filled with old pine cones—maybe the one Doc had hid in—then lifted up over the crest through blowdowns. The lodgepole was so big and shadowing in here, and the little blue spruce growing up under their branches, that you hardly felt the rain at all. In the dampness, the forest smelled sweet; chips of rotted pine were floating in puddles, and the tiny aspen no bigger than a bush were shuddering water pearls off their fragile leaves. Eddie happened to glance up, and on a branch ahead of him sat a grouse; he looked like a little old man hunched up with an umbrella on his head. Eddie pretended to shoot at him, then grinned because damn if that grouse didn't wink an eye at him before tucking his head down on his shoulder again.

Then Eddie became conscious of something strange. There were no other birds about. Oh, they were there all right, but like the grouse they'd hunkered down, silent. Almost at the same instant Eddie realized the forest was too quiet, Lester snapped up his head and snorted. Eddie swung around in the saddle. Joline was next in line, slouched over on his horse; then came the packhorse, and behind it the two other Game and Fish boys. Joline started to say something, seeing Eddie turn, but Eddie put his finger to his lips. He pointed ahead. Something up there. With his eyes, Joline asked, What? Eddie shrugged. He didn't know. For a moment there was no sound but the sluff of the horses' feet or a rasp when a pine branch would scrape the canvas that was covering the elk carcass.

Now Lester was shivering and peering on both sides of

the trail into the dark timber. Just ahead, the trail cut into a fairly steep sidehill that led down to a creek. The timber was slightly smaller in here, but tight-spaced new second-growth trees. Lester stumbled as he hit on the sidehill trail, no more than a foot and a half wide. Then he snorted and froze. Below Eddie, in the bottom near the creek, was a monstrous black object. It was partly screened by willows and tree trunks. Eddie could only see a black slab side of it. Bear, he thought. But now, because Eddie had stopped short, one of the Game and Fish horses butted against Lester who gave a jump, lost his footing on the wet slick trail, and clunked around to get his hooves set again. By the time Eddie glanced back down, the animal had moved. "Holy smoke!," Joline breathed. "Willya look at that!"

It was a bull moose. Eddie had seen hundreds of them in his life, from the yearlings, yellow-legged and spindly, to the old graybacks, with their snouts gone thin and their teeth worn out. He'd shot moose and eaten them, roped a few, and ran many others off his meadows in winter. And he'd been charged and run by moose, had tracked them and watched them breed; seen old cows in the spring plunge into icy water, come out with their hides frozen silver; and yet, ten minutes later, be lying in the greening willows, licking a smoking calf. Eddie had even seen a moose smash the porch window of his house at the ranch. But he'd never seen one like this.

The animal was a spectacle, a presence like another human being suddenly discovered. Eddie and the wardens were stock-still on the trail, maybe fifty feet above the moose. His head had lifted now and was jerking slightly left, then right, as he tried to see what he was winding. Moose don't have very good eyesight, but those mule ears and sensitive nose made up for it. Just then, the moose blew out a snort that rattled through the young timber and echoed off like a bugle. His giant forefoot slapped down, kicking back a spray of pine needles and dirt. For an instant, Eddie saw his great black and humped shoulder rise, that is, the hair on it rose, stiffened, and his teeth glinted bared. Then up he came, head lowered in the charge.

The confrontation hadn't taken ten seconds, but in that time, a small thought had ticked in the back of Eddie's mind: suppose the bull decides to take this trail? A very narrow trail, where a horse couldn't turn around on the sidehill, and, even if he did, four other horses were jammed in behind him. Lester had just realized the same thing; now, trembling, he was trying to back on the trail, while below him, closing the distance, crashing up, came a black thunder, the teeth still bared, the big forefeet flailing ahead of him. And then that rack of horn, it was tossed back on the moose's shoulders, the horns a tawny yellow and white reaching out like monstrous arms, the fingers enormous shovels and spines. To Eddie, the rack looked as big as the cowcatcher on a locomotive, and the remarkable thing was that in lunging through the timber, never once did the moose hook a horn on a tree. Eddie couldn't believe it. He watched frozen as the monster crashed toward him.

"Get back!" Joline cried. "Turn, Eddie, he's taking us!" And the young warden shouting, "Christ, my horse has stepped over the rope—"

Eddie never had a chance to turn, so fascinated and stunned was he by the suddenness of the charge. There was a panic: lashing of hooves, hollers of men. Eddie felt Lester rearing to get up the sidehill, off the trail, but he never made it; Eddie knew he wouldn't. Eddie leaped off him and went rolling downhill, almost into the front feet of the moose. Eddie was turning over and over, seeing a snatch of the rainy sky, then pine needles. The earth was shaking because another horse had thumped down, Joline and the Game and Fish men shouting at each other. Then Eddie rolled into a tree about twenty feet down the slope, and, when he scrambled to his feet, the moose was gone.

Looking up, Eddie had to chuckle. The men from the

Game and Fish Department were on foot now, the horses loose in a stomping riot and terror combined. Lester— failing to climb the steep hillside, the dumb son-of-a-bitch— had now got himself about ten feet out the ledge trail, turned around bassackwards and whimpering in his eyes for Eddie to come straighten him out. Meanwhile, Joline Roush was scraping himself up off the edge of the slope. The packhorse had almost bucked the elk off, fallen down, and was now lying pinched against a tree with the boy warden kicking him in the butt trying to get him up. And the other Game and Fish kid in his red shirt was the only one who seemed to have survived the charge. He was squatting on the topside of the trail, looking up at the ragged rainy skyline. He had his camera in front of his face, and, when Eddie came up beside him, there was a silver flash, then another.

On the crest of the ridge, having pretty well wiped out the intruders, stood the bull moose, silhouetted against the sky. A portrait, he was indeed, with his rack raised proud and his big wattle hanging at least a foot down from his chin. By now, Eddie could see fully the size of him: Lester was 15.2 hands, and that moose was every bit as big; in fact, he could have gone a good sixteen hands at the withers. He wasn't old, despite his size; his hair jet black and strong, in the prime of life, Eddie thought. While Eddie watched him, and the Game and Fish kid snapped, the moose looked back down at them in a lordly sort of way, as if telling them: don't try that trail again when I'm around. Then slowly, not showing any fear, he simply slid off the skyline. A few moments later, the sun hazed out from behind a raincloud, and the birds were cheeping again.

"By God," the boy warden whispered, "that was something."

"I got three pictures of him, gotta be good ones," said the kid. "If I wasn't so surprised, I could have got another while he was charging Eddie. Damn, you were lucky, Eddie, your horse got a whiff of him coming and went right over backwards."

"It wasn't no ideal place to meet him," Eddie said, "but I'm sure glad I had the chance."

Joline was standing hands on his hips, looking up toward the ridge where the moose had been. "That has got to be the largest Shiras in existence. And I've seen a lot of 'em."

"He's pretty damn good," the boy warden added.

"A record," Joline said softly. "I'll bet that rack will top the Boone and Crockett right now; and the depth of shoulder on him, in sheer size, he's bigger than anything I've ever run across. What about you, Eddie?"

"He can do her all."

Joline grinned wryly. "You had him hid out back here, I suppose? Kind of putting him on ice, were you?"

Eddie was turning Lester around on the trail, didn't answer for a moment. And he wasn't just sure how much he wanted to tell Joline. Finally, Joline repeated the question. "Naw," Eddie said, "I ain't run onto him before, and that's pretty close to the truth. But I did know about him."

"Tracks?"

Eddie nodded.

Joline swung slowly onto his horse. "There's a lot of hunters who'd pay a fortune for a trophy like that."

"You got some moose hunters coming?" asked the boy warden.

"Naw," Eddie said.

The boy warden looked at Joline. "Well, I imagine there's quite a few that'd like to be coming back in here, if they knew about him."

"If they knew," Eddie said, "but they don't." He caught Joline's eyes, and the boy warden's too, before he thumped Lester off, and they started back down the sidehill trail.

One thing Eddie never had much time to do was fish. But late that afternoon, waiting for Doll to come home from the clinic, Eddie walked over to Moon Creek where it twisted through the meadow. Coming back down from the Sink, Eddie had noticed a helluva nice brookie finning out here; so now with an old bamboo fly rod a dude had given him twenty years before, Eddie slipped up on the creek, planning to lay his first fly in the big still pool. Damn! He hit and snagged the tall grass alongside the creek. Out of practice. Jerked her loose, then squatted again, and the sing of the fly line sounded good in the late afternoon, with the sun slanting down and the grass fresh from the rain. He dropped the fly in the pool, let it drift until he couldn't see it under the bank. Waited for the slap. But no sound. Slowly, he began to retrieve. But the fly had snagged. Eddie swore. Now he'd have to walk over to the pool and spook everything in it while he got his line loose. But as he stood up, the line came alive and sucked away from him. He chortled like a boy, held the rod aloft and approached the pool. There was a slap of water, a heavy insulting tug on the rod. Then Eddie could see the green back and flashing speckled sides of the beautiful brook. Two and a half pounds anyhow, which was good for this stream. As he peered down into the deep crystal hole, watching the fish dive, he saw a second brook as big or bigger, swimming beside the first as if it might pluck the fly out of its mouth.

Eddie got a look at the jaw on the other fish; it was long and underslung like a salmon, obviously an old male, protecting his hole and maybe now before spawning season making room for a female. When Eddie finally hauled the brookie up on the grass, he didn't even touch her with his hand. She was bulging, a big sleek female surely with a bellyful of eggs. Eddie just admired her in the sun; then holding the hook by the barb wriggled her off it, and she flopped back free. Eddie had looked forward to eating trout tonight, but hell, there'd be another time. It wasn't really the eating of 'em, or the catching either that made Eddie love fishing; it was just . . . well, maybe Eddie was like some

Indian afraid of starving: he just had to prove that he *could* catch 'em if he needed to. Meanwhile, they were there, friends of his; no point disturbing their life unless he had to. It was kind of comforting to see game or fish, and maybe this was the first time he'd ever really explained it to himself: that it must have been an urge that went way back.

Another of the damn primitive hangovers was the shoeing of horses; Eddie'd hated it from boyhood. But now, when Doll's pickup still hadn't driven in and the sun was almost burning into the quaker ridge on the other side of the valley, Eddie walked back over to the log barn, got out his shoeing tools. Then he wrangled a couple of geldings he was going to work into his pack string for fall hunting. The first one was a roan named Smiley. He had a wild white look in his eye like, If you touch me, brother, with that rasp I'm going to tear this barn down. Eddie hooked on the halter ropes on both sides, then spoke to Smiley a few words, finally grabbed ahold of his front hoof. As Eddie twisted the hoof around to start rasping, he looked up because there was a shadow over the door. Doll.

"Hadn't better stand right there," Eddie said. "In case this broomie throws a fit, he'd like to fall right over on you."

"I shouldn't be out here," Doll said. "I really ought to go in and fix dinner. But I wanted to hear about you. Did you find the elk?"

"Yas."

Doll leaned against the log door jamb. She still had her nursing uniform on, her cap perched a little cockeyed on her ruff of reddish hair. "Oh, Eddie, I just can't believe they'd take your permit."

"Well, now I wouldn't be shoeing horses if I thought they was," Eddie said. "They're bluffing. Stand still, you son-of-a-bitch!" Smiley was twisting on the halter, trying to pull his hoof loose from Eddie's grip. Once, Eddie thought, he'd been strong enough to about break a horse's ankle off. But now it was all he could do to hold on and rasp at the same time. He took about five passes across the hoof, smoothed it out some; by now Smiley was sagging into him. Eddie's back ached where he'd rolled down the sidehill, and he had a crick in his neck. He let Smiley's hoof go, straightened up painfully. Then he sucked in a gulp of breath and leaned against the side of the hay rack.

Doll had come into the barn now, edged past Smiley. "You'd think," she said softly, "it's about time you quit smoking."

"Yas, yas."

"Your wind isn't any good. Your brother died of emphysema."

Eddie grinned. "Hell, honey, he just got old and tired of shoeing horses."

"Well I'm tired too." Doll murmured. Then she reached into the hay rack, grabbed a few green stalks, and began twisting them together like a rope. She nodded at Smiley. "Turn him loose, Eddie."

"I ain't done."

"They're not going to let you hunt. It's all over town. They're going to make an example of you, and it's perfectly legal if they do. After all, it's your second offense."

"The other wasn't my fault neither!" Eddie flared. "Three years ago, a goddamned mixup over a dude's limit of fish."

"I know. But I just got thinking, driving out from town . . . maybe this is all a blessing. We're . . . " she stared at the rope of hay in her hands . . . "we're both getting finished here, Eddie. Made our lives, the kids are gone. Getting tired of shoeing horses."

Eddie didn't look at her. He'd lifted up his boot and was tapping some mud off the heel; it didn't need cleaning, but it kind of kept him from listening. "And then?" he said finally.

"Susan called today. She was so bubbly and sweet. Just wanted to know how we were. And Eddie, she's moved into a new house of her own, small place, right on the beach.

She's dying for us to come out to California. And particularly after I told her about this Game and Fish mess. She just begged us to come."

"And not come back?" Eddie murmured.

"No. Not come back. Oh sure, in summers we would. And we'd come visit Ly and Darlene in hunting season. But the rest of the time, we'd be out there as a family, more or less, what's left of it, and making a new life."

"Doing, for God's sake, what?" Eddie's head snapped up; he flung the file with a rattle into his shoeing tools. "I didn't figure you'd start this lecture again. Not with what's been going on."

"It was Susan calling."

"It's all the time now, Doll. Your heart ain't in this ranch no more. Sure, you got your nursing, you been a few places; you and Susan could buddy up out there; you'd be working and having a chance to do all them things you talk about, musicales and museums and liberries and God knows what all. So I say go. G'wan. Go out there. Tell your sawbones in the clinic you ain't coming back. Just stay."

"Eddie . . ."

She came to him and gripped him hard. His face was wizened up tight. "Can you see me out there?" he muttered.

"I can see you trying, Eddie. Trying something new."

"This is all I know."

"And it's ending! That's what you got to realize. We're seeing it every day. They're phasing you out like a steam locomotive. But Eddie, we've still got some good years together. If we sold this place, we'd have enough to live on, use the time we have, enjoy it for a change, not just work like mules."

Eddie looked at her. There were tears in her eyes. He said, "It's been a long time for you, ain't it?" And he nodded as if convincing himself. Then he eased past her and around Smiley's rump to the door; he could see across the old logs of the corrals to the meadows and then into the cliff of black timber on the east side of the valley. But he was seeing more than scenery: little things like a new door he'd cut into a haycrib or a headgate on the main ditch. When was that, 1934? Or 1949, when he'd rewrapped with burlap that pipe going into the corral tank? Everyplace he looked he'd see some pissant job of carpentering or digging or splicing with baling wire, something done with his hands. Each job was like a spike driven into a calendar day, and a few rusty nails or old boards were all he ever had to show at the end of thousands of days—and his father before him, all they had to show were these rude log buildings, a swatch of valley that didn't grow much hay, and the tired old black mule.

Doll was standing next to him, her head on his shoulder. Maybe she'd seen the same nails, for she'd driven some of them. Eddie said, "I ain't gonna figure it out yet, Doll. Mainly because I don't know how. But I reckon you better go if Susan wants you. You need a vacation."

"I don't want to leave you."

"If you're thinking of settling out there, you damn well better look first," Eddie grunted.

"I suppose so." Then brightening, Doll told him to leave the horse and come on in. She'd fix something for supper.

"I'll be right along." Eddie said. But it wasn't that quick. He did shoe Smiley, hammered the hell out of all four feet, like now the pain of blacksmithing, or the memory, was something he'd better hold onto.

CHAPTER 3

"THERE ain't a rancher in this country," said Jake Galusha, Eddie's neighbor, "that don't think sometimes about selling out. And you give it a few years, Eddie, there'll be just a handful of us left, and that includes outfitters too."

"Well, what'll be here?" Eddie said.

Galusha lay a pinch of snuff into his lip. "New towns, cabins, them tourist home tracts, or just more goddamned national forests and public toilets. I been to Colorado, Eddie. You ought to see it down there: every valley's got a metropolis in it. We'll all be gone, Eddie."

"To where, though?"

Galusha glanced at him. "Ain't that the hell of it?" He sucked the snuff, spat it out in an arch, and Eddie never did get an answer, because, for him and Jake Galusha, there really was none.

Strange thing about it, Eddie reflected, life had been so simple starting out. He wondered where it had come off the track. Take Yancey, Eddie's dad . . . and sometimes when Eddie was low he'd think about old Yance and wonder what he would have done. For, in Yancey's day, you went and grabbed what you wanted; there weren't wardens or outsiders or regulations telling you what to do. You took up ground; with your own sweat you turned it into your rocks and your trees, and—as Yance used to say with a grin—"If you worked hard enough, you lived till you died."

Yance did, anyhow. In January 1941, Yance was eighty-two but still out with the team and sleigh feeding the few cattle he had. Eddie hadn't been home long; for three years he'd been bumming around the country, driving a truck, working on an oil rig. After quitting school at seventeen, Eddie didn't know what to do with himself, except get drunk and howl a bit and fight when it came up. Anyhow, after three years on the road, Eddie came home for Christmas and found that the ranch had pretty well fallen apart.

Doc was supposed to be running it, but while Eddie'd been gone, Doc had had another attack of his coughing and ended up tending bar down at Green River City. Just what bartending had to do with rehabilitation, Eddie never figured out. But Doc was on a veteran's pension for having been gassed in France in World War I, and he claimed this job had been suggested by the government doctors—less outdoor exercise. You couldn't believe Doc; he'd turned out pretty windy since his famous war experiences, which he'd got a lot of practice telling about in saloons.

Well, Doc being in Green River City had worried Eddie's mother (she was only Doc's stepmother but had a heart big enough for any waif, the scragglier the better). So, after Christmas, Eddie's ma had gone down to Green River City to attend some church function having to do with Bible classes, etc. She would travel the state for several weeks, looking in on Doc when she could, and, in short, getting out of the worst and coldest time of the winter up at the ranch. That's when she'd asked Eddie, begged him, to stay with his pop for a few weeks. Of course, at the ranch they were snowed in all winter. Getting out meant snowshoeing five miles and hoping you'd run onto Ben McElwee clinking down his snow road with his dog team, carrying the mail.

So on that January morning of 1941, like every other since Eddie'd been home, Yance crawled up on the big haystack and forked down a green, sweet smelling mound, which Eddie spread around on the sleigh. Eddie should have been on the stack himself; pitching was the hard part, but no, by God, old Yance said Eddie didn't know how to take the stack apart properly; snow'd get in there and rot the hay. Yance said, "The best way for a man to keep things going like he wants is to do it himself."

Standing on the stack with his coveralls caked with snow and ice, his hawk nose and fierce sunken eyes scowling down on Eddie, old Yance looked like a silvered scarecrow, flung up on the stack all crooked and bony. Hell, at eighty-two, a strong wind could have blown him away. Yet he was tough and cranky, God how he'd nicknack at Eddie all day long. But, somehow, that morning, old Yance was digging hay and flashing his fork up into the sun; it was just cold enough to be crystal clear, bone dry with the snow glistening like rock salt and the lodgepoles on the side of the valley dusted blue-white and sparkling. You could hear the sound of a branch snap for miles. Old Yance was sucking that pure air in his dribbling nose and sprying himself around the stack like a boy again.

Then Eddie felt the sleigh jerk; the team bucked forward, threw their heads. Eddie whirled just in time to see Yance sinking down in the snow beside the sleigh. He had toppled over backwards off the stack; Eddie didn't know why, lost his footing or what. But he struck the hard frozen edge of the sleigh with his back, and when Eddie got to him, the old man was coughing and writhing in the snow. Eddie put his arms around him, tried to drag him up sitting. The old man's head fell forward; there was spittle running down the sides of his mouth where the tobacco had stained. He was breathing so hard and raspy Eddie thought he was going to die in his arms.

The old man carried a bottle of rye whisky in a saddlebag on the hayrack. The first thing he croaked was, "Get it!" Eddie took the bottle and inserted in into that hawky face, the whiskey slobbering down onto the old man's neckerchief. But he must have got some in the spout for a moment or two, for Yance shook himself like a dog after a swim. "Jesus Christ!" he rattled. Then, grabbing Eddie's arm, he pulled himself up.

"You lie on the sleigh, Pop, I'll haul you in."

The gaunt face swung to Eddie. Yance always wore a cloth hat and wrapped a black scarf around from his chin to the top of his head. It made him look like a beaky old raven. "You ain't hauling me no place. We feed the load first. That's what we do."

"For God's sake, Pop. You like to busted your back."

Yance had creaked himself up onto the sleigh, then crawled to the log front where the reins were tied. He pulled himself up like an animal that had lost the use of its legs. And with his skinny arms wrapped over the log front of the sleigh, he told the team: "Hup!" The team plodded around the feedground, Eddie forking off the hay to the cows, dreading to glance up at his father, sure he'd be croaked there and hanging like a skeleton. But sure enough, that's how they went home, Yance still hanging on. Eddie had to carry him into the cabin. It was then he knew Yance was going to die.

The cabin had been fixed up pretty nice with new linoleum and paneling since Eddie and Doll had lived in it. But in those days, it was still just rough logs Yance had whacked square. There was a parlor you came into, with Yance's old rocker in front of the fireplace; off to the left was the woodstove, where Eddie's ma cooked, pots hanging above it. Beyond, around a crooked little corner and lower so you had to stoop, were two bedrooms, one where Yance and Eddie's ma lived and the other for Eddie or whatever kid or visitor was there. There was no electricity, just gas lamps; and the old logs of the walls were smoky and dark. Yance had never had time to taxiderm like Eddie, so, for decorations, he just hung up things like bear traps and old buffalo guns; he also had some Indian lances and a war shield; and, then, in dark little pictures, even back to tintypes, there marched the history of his life on a rough pine shelf next to the chimney.

First thing Eddie did was stir up the fire and try to get the old man in bed. But now Yance's skin was dry, and he was shivering feverish. His eyes got wandering, rolling like they weren't connected in his head anymore. Eddie finally got a buffalo robe laid over him. Then Eddie said, "Pop, I'm going out on snowshoes after the doctor."

But the old man wasn't listening. Or he was someplace else and going to leave it quick; he knew that. Eddie got him more whiskey, propped him up in the big iron-framed bed. And now Yance's eyes burned soft and distant under his high forehead. Strange thing, one time a writer fellow had been in Beaver, heard about old Yance, the pioneer, and wanted to "put down his story." But Yance wouldn't even meet him. "What's done is done," he had said when asked about his life, that's all Eddie knew, till now.

Like an old Indian chief burying his ponies with him, Yance seemed to draw in the people and memories from those faded pictures on the shelf as he told Eddie whatever he could remember of his life. Of course, it came out disjointed, not making much sense; but from what Eddie had heard later from his mother, he put it together that Yance had been born in 1859, somewhere in Kansas.

First memory Yance had was Rebel border gangs whooping into town and shooting it up. When the Civil War was over, the Bulwer family came west in a wagon, settled in Nevada. There, after some years, Yance's father was forced to shoot a man over a water dispute. He wasn't convicted of murder, just advised to move on. Yance and his family must have split then, for Yance ended up working in the mines in Deadwood, South Dakota. Then in 1879, he joined the army and chased Indians in Wyoming and Montana for three years.

How he ended up in the Beaver country Eddie never knew, except later an old timer had claimed that Yance came into the Beaver country rounding up wild horses. A party of Shoshones caught him and his partner and, along the Beaver river, began roasting their feet in the coals. Fortunately, the Shoshones had found whiskey in Yance's packs; presently, they got more interested in drinking than torturing. Old Yance made his escape in darkness and walked out nearly eighty miles. His partner died on the way. Now as the old man lay under the buffalo robe he told Eddie to put out the fire on his feet.

Anyhow, Yance had seen the Beaver country and must have decided to settle. For a few years, he drove a jerkline freight team across the Red Desert; then he blacksmithed and made a living as a wolfer, breaking up the packs that were killing so many sheep and cattle in those days. Finally, he located the first homestead, filed on it; then his brother Perce showed up from someplace. Perce threw in with him, and later Perce's wife; they kept adding their 160 acre homesteads until they had the full 640 on Moon Creek, the gateway into the basin.

Yance's first marriage was in 1894, to Maud Allyn of Ogden, Utah. He brought her to the homestead cabin (by now Perce and his family had sold out to Yance and moved on); Maud and Yance had three infants, all of whom died before Dwayne (Doc) lived, and then Cyril. When Maud died in 1915, Yance lived on alone at the homestead until winter of 1918, when he took a trip out to Omaha on the railroad to sell his few cattle. It was here that he met Polly Deevers; she was waiting tables in the Grand Union Hotel. He brought her back to the homestead like Maud before her, and poor Polly, half Yance's age and twice as civilized, cried for months in the isolation and rudeness of the life. But soon Eddie was born, Polly's only child; then Yance got to grubbing out more meadows and adding cows.

Eddie could see, even growing up, that there wasn't enough in cows to make a living. But the way Yance bullwhacked the outfit, they managed to get by all those years; first Doc leaving to the war, then Cyril, and finally Eddie alone, doing all the chores. It seemed to Eddie like his whole life had been spent huddling in front of that wood stove after milking cows in the dark, then harnessing the team with that frozen stiff leather, later snowshoeing out to his trap lines. Eddie's mother taught him the first six grades of school, there in the log parlor where his father was now dying.

That day in January 1941, Eddie sat beside the bed and then sat on it for the whole long arch of the sun as it passed over the valley, burning the snow and laying blinding shafts of light into the cabin. Old Yancey rattled and coughed and whispered and dreamed. No, there wasn't anything remarkable in his life; he was just one of those who passed through and didn't ask no medals for his hardship. After all, what he'd got back from it was freedom, a piece of ground that was his and not a creditor in the world. And maybe more. Old Yance had, as he'd said, "seen the elephant." Eddie had thought this referred to coming west in a covered wagon. But that afternoon he was led to believe it meant more. It was a brave man knowing he had faced all the terror there was in life—and no more peril, suffering, or loneliness was to be his.

Toward evening, the wind started to blow; the cabin door rattled where Yance had told Eddie to fix it, but Eddie's carpentering was pretty sorry in those days. Then the cabin windows got gray as slate and finally silver black. Eddie sat there on the iron bed with his arm locked around Yance like he was a little boy, hoping Yance would be telling him Indian tales. For the first time then, Eddie began to cry, let the big tears come splashing down. He'd hated old Yance, fought him, quit him after the drudgery work of so many years. And yet sitting there hugging him as his lights went slowly out, Eddie knew Yance, in his way, had loved him best of all the boys. And loved the land and passed it on to him. That's what Yance's life had meant, and that was about all.

Yet even going out he was still tough. Cantankerous old bugger wouldn't arrange to die when they could bury him. The ground was froze up tight. So Eddie made a coffin, and, after all the mourning and the ceremony in town was over, they hauled him back on a sleigh, Eddie and his mother and Doc; they set Yance in the barn until spring; and when the ground thawed in May, they dug him in by Moon Creek where it curved toward the corrals. They had a pretty flossy headstone carved. On it was the one poem anybody had ever heard old Yance say, and nobody knew who it came from or where. It went:

> When all the world was young, lad,
> And all the trees were green.
> When all the geese were swans, lad,
> And every lass a queen . . .

They hadn't but got Yance buried before Eddie was fighting with Doc. Seemed like Doc's lungs had healed, or at least somebody'd got to him drinking and gave him an idea. Anyhow, he came beating up to the ranch in a new Ford truck with all his belongings in the back. He'd come home for good, he said. He was going to get rid of the cattle Yance had; in fact, they were already sold; Doc figured to turn the place into a resort for hunters and fishermen. Well, Eddie by now had been running the ranch, and somehow after that last day with his father, he figured it was his, knowing he and Yance had the same love for it.

But Doc had a dark, mean side to him and also some trashy buggers for friends. They'd got to drinking one night when Eddie came in from moving cows; words followed, Eddie's mother tugging them apart and even finally getting a shotgun and holding it on them. Well, that settled the argument for a half hour or so. Then Doc, weaving surly drunk, followed Eddie out to the meathouse. "You got a chance," Doc slurred, "to come in with me, and I'll teach you. Or you can get out."

"I wouldn't come into hell with you," Eddie said. That's when Doc picked up a meat hook and flung it at him.

A few minutes later, Doc was lying out on the grass bleeding from the mouth and ears; Eddie had hauled him from the meathouse. Then he went in and told his mother goodbye. Over her wailing and the growls of Doc's drunk friends, Eddie wallopped his few belongings together, took two horses, the one he was riding and a packhorse, and rode out of the valley south toward Beaver. But didn't stop there. He picked up a job out in the desert in spring roundup, working for Mr. Tolley Archibald.

This was a big outfit, and Tolley, like old Yance, had a hard streak in him when it came to hazing new men. One day he and Eddie were out riding alone, near the Sand Springs water hole, when Eddie did some dumb thing like leaving a gate down in the trap and a steer got out. Tolley went after the steer and finally run him back in. Then he looked at Eddie. He was a big man, dust streaks on his face and a cruel kind of mustache that curled down. Slowly, Tolley took out the revolver he always carried. He didn't point it at Eddie but just held it there. "I heard you were a stupid kid," Tolley said, "but I never dreamed you'd insult me like you have."

"Well . . . ," Eddie flustered, "what have I done . . . ?"

Tolley's face got purple dark. "You know damn well, kid. Now turn around and start riding."

"What?"

"I'm going to kill you."

Eddie couldn't believe it. There he was, riding side by side with Tolley, who was laying his revolver across his left arm and pointing it at Eddie's belly. Tolley never said a word, but Eddie knew they were going to some execution point, probably an alkali quicksand that would make it look like Eddie'd got trapped in there. At first, in the slow shuffle of the horses, Eddie was shivering scared. After all, Mr. Archibald was a big man in the county, old timer; he could do what he wanted. But then, slowly, a stinging mad rose in Eddie's eyes. He hadn't done nothing, and, if the man was going to kill him for nothing, then he'd better start right now. With that, Eddie made a leap across, striking that revolver first and it spun away, then he and Tolley Archibald crashing onto the hard desert. Eddie had him by the throat and was beating his skull on the ground, Tolley screaming, "I was only kidding you. It's a joke!"

Finally, Eddie let him up; the older man was pale as silk, his cheek bruised where Eddie'd decked him, and he kept rubbing his throat, hoarsely trying to explain.

"You git on your horse," Eddie snapped. He jerked the gun at him, and Mr. Tolley Archibald scrambled back on. Then Eddie rode beside him with the revolver held at his temple, rode Mr. Tolley Archibald into the Archibald Land and Cattle cow camp, where there must have been thirty-five cowhands and a fencing crew assembled. And Tolley shouting to his foreman: "Will you tell this crazy bastard I was only kidding him!"

That's all it was, Eddie found out sheepishly: Tolley's way of hazing. He had a world of practical jokes, it seemed, but maybe Eddie had lived too far back from civilization; it wasn't funny to him. After roundup was done, the Archibalds said they had no more work, and Eddie drifted on.

All that saved him from being a tramp-line rider was Pearl Harbor. Eddie was in a roadside diner in Utah, hitchhiking to California, when he heard the news. He like to threw his arms in the air; in fact, he did hug the waitress, and everybody in the diner thought he was nuts. The thing was, Eddie'd toyed with joining the army for months now, but every time he'd get hungry enough to want to enlist, he'd stop into some ranch and get hired on for a few weeks, and the urge for steady work would go away. But now it seemed to him that you'd have to go; you had a score to settle with them Japs. More than this, it'd be a clean break with the past, because all back there—up in Beaver—family and home were over and done now.

Eddie enlisted in the Marine Corps on Christmas Eve 1941. He was a private, of course. He got out a private, August 1945; medical discharge and a pension. In between, a mountain kid died and a man came home; never quite the same after that. He'd dream about it for long years. Maybe now he understood Doc a little better, even if Doc's war stories had just been windies made up in some saloon.

But Eddie's, that he'd rarely told, were real. He'd seen his own kind of elephant out there among the shattered coconut palms, the land crabs, and the jungle rot. Eddie had started at Guadalcanal; for some reason they'd stuck him in Marine Engineers. He wasn't an engineer; building bridges and setting up campsites just rubbed him wrong. A rifle was more what he knew. To most fellows it was the reverse; they'd just as leave get out of a rifle company or at least get on a machine gun. Not Eddie. He'd always loved to hunt, and his wartime goal was to get into a scout and sniper team, which seemed to him to combine hunting and independence and enough excitement to keep the time passing.

Eddie got his wish and became one of the oldest scout-snipers who survived; went from the beginning at Guadalcanal to the end at Okinawa, with stops along the way. He got hit by a Jap knee mortar on Bougainville, a few fragments in the butt. That was easy, earned him a couple of months in New Zealand; he spent a lot of this rehabilitation time up in the lake area by Rotorua, hunting deer and fishing. But they got him back in time for Guam. In the moonlight, on Orote Peninsula, second night ashore, the Japs launched a banzai against the Orote airfield. Eddie was on point in a hole closest to the mangrove swamp where the Japs were drinking sake, shouting curses, and forming their charge. He had a machine gunner with him, and, when the gunner was killed, Eddie took over, then ran out of ammunition and hid in the hole. The Japs were leaping across him like goblins in the moon, their equipment clanking; they were drunk, howling banzais. By now, most of the fleet in the bay and marine artillery ashore had zeroed in on the charge area, and Eddie's hole was in the center of the barrage field. Once, he tried to get up and run, but the earth was shaking in gigantic flashes, hunks of steel flicking, hissing through the air, and, in the brilliant electric flashes, Eddie could see Jap bodies and arms and legs floating up toward the moon.

When the barrage ended, there was just wails and moaning out across the wrecked trees and churned up earth. Eddie could see Japs crawling back toward the swamp like crippled snakes; a few were bolt upright trying to walk over the shellholes, their eyes wild, and their mouths hanging open. It was like looking at an elk or moose, shot in the back, trying to drag itself away. Watching in horror, Eddie crawled out of his hole and found a Jap rifle and ammo belt. Then he began to fire at the retreating Nips, killing as many as he could, putting them out of their misery. When dawn came up and the field was quiet again and smoking in the stink of flesh, a Marine colonel in dungarees ran over to Eddie, pulled him up from his hole. They hadn't believed anybody could have survived out there. A week later, at the old marine barracks on Guam, Eddie was awarded the Navy Cross.

When Guam was done, Eddie's outfit went back to Guadalcanal to train for the next landing. Hell, Eddie had had two years of training by now. Maneuvers were a pain in the ass and, moreover, made him sad. For there were only a few left like Eddie; his old friends from the first days were shot out or gone home because of wounds. Eddie had a hunch that he better get out himself while his luck was still good. But still and all, he was a buck sergeant now and had his own scout-sniper team. The colonel b.s'd him into staying for just one more show. Turned out to be Okinawa. Eddie's team fought its way through Naha, house to house; he was so God-awful tired by then, the fighting seemed to go on, week after week.

One day, on the south part of the island . . . a bright sunny day on the green hills, the platoon leader pointed Eddie toward one of the tombs. They were big concrete faced bulges built into the sides of the hills; supposed to represent a woman's womb, Eddie was told, and the mouth of it was a narrow little door. The radio said there were Japs holed up in here; they often used the tombs to fight out of. Eddie and two other boys crawled up to the mouth of the tomb to try to lay a satchel charge in it, blow it. Just then, a little Jap wearing eyeglasses came scurrying out with his arms raised high. From the red stripes on his collar, he was an officer of some kind, but he didn't look sixteen. Eddie, crouching there beside the rock wall, was only three or four feet from him. Strangely, the Jap was holding his rifle above his head, in his upraised arms. Hell, Eddie thought: he's so green he probably don't know how to surrender.

Well, he did know how; and Eddie, in dogtiredness, had got too slow. It only took a flash of a second for the Jap to edge out the tomb door, see Eddie; then, in a wild slash swung the rifle butt. Eddie's forearm broke some of the blow, but the rest caught him on the jaw and throat. He went down coughing, blood and teeth coming out of his mouth; and the Jap was pulling his legs, trying to drag him into the tomb, use him as a hostage maybe. But Eddie by now was woozing in and out of consciousness. A BAR was slamming, bullets chipping off the door stones, singing away, and Eddie writhed there for a time until finally the mouth of the tomb was quiet dark, and Eddie had been pulled out by his partners beyond the wall.

They propped him up there in safety; a corpsman came and tried to swab at Eddie's mouth and bleeding teeth. Eddie could hardly talk in the pain of it, and in the blind mad that he'd let that Nip come so close and hadn't killed him on sight. Then the lieutenant, a young scared kid, scurried up beside Eddie at the wall. "Well," the lieutenant said, "what are you going to do? They're still in there."

"You get me a flamethrower," Eddie said.

The lieutenant, who was in his first fight, seemed pleased by that; Eddie showed initiative, yessir. But Eddie in his head wasn't showing anything but a kind of animal hate, so tired and in so much pain that if he killed somebody else that'd be fine, and if he killed himself with 'em that'd be fine too; at least it would bring the goddamned suffering to an end.

Eddie picked up the flamethrower and started to run.

"Christ!" the lieutenant hollered. "Not straight on. Drop down from above!"

Half staggering with the flamethrower on his back, Eddie stumbled directly across the concrete patio toward the tomb door. The other scout-snipers were hanging on the hillside above the tomb; that was the way Eddie should have gone, where they couldn't shoot at you. But hell, he was asking to be killed, everyone knew that. And he stood swaying in front of the door, which was only about four feet high and a couple wide.

Eddie rammed the snout of the flamethrower through the door, turned on the gas. The great licking tongue blew inside; Eddie was crooked around the edge of the doorway, shielding himself from the heat of it, and there was no sound but the roaring flame, smoke pouring out into Eddie's face, finally getting so bad and so stinking that Eddie had a fit of coughing. Then he was kneeling there crying. And the lieutenant and a whole bunch of them, they were around Eddie. A photographer too. The flamethrower had long ago been shut off. But the stink was still there.

Coming now, single file out of the tomb, their arms raised, were Okinawan women and children, those still alive.

They were badly burned, black slabs hanging bubbling from their arms, faces, necks, breasts: brown naked kids, clothes singed off, big bellies burned, kids trying to whimper, and their mothers slapping them to shut 'em up. And, finally, they were hauling out the little Jap who'd hit Eddie. The flamethrower had burned him about to bones. He was the only soldier in the tomb. Eddie had burned seventy-six women, children, and old men, more than half of them dead.

"You didn't know they were in there," the lieutenant kept telling Eddie. "How could you have known?"

Eddie just sat there, rocking back and forth on his knees, asking himself what in Christ's name was it all for?

Nobody ever answered his question, of course, but when it came to where he could remember asking it, he was on the deck of a hospital ship churning slowly east across the Pacific. The war was over now, they told him. Seemed like they had him drugged about half the time, and they were operating on his jaw to get the lump out of it and refit some false teeth. Eddie heard one of the other patients wisecracking that the big marine with a beard, he's psycho. And Eddie guessed he was. By the time he hit the West Coast, he'd had a liberty in Honolulu, where he'd gotten roaring drunk, smashed apart a Jap whorehouse (massage parlor they called them). And there was more damn commotion in San Francisco, chasing women and fighting shore patrols. The killer instinct, or whatever the hell it was, still bursted out of Eddie for months to come; maybe marked him for life, he didn't know. To calm him down, they finally had to take his stripes away, which they said was too bad, and they discharged him with his medals December 20, 1945. Almost four full years dropped out of his life. And homesick now, he got on a train for Green River City, Wyoming.

A blizzard was howling down through the buttes when Eddie blew in there. He went to the saloon where Doc had worked and found some of Doc's old buddies. They pulled off Eddie's green issue coat, saw his medals. By God they wanted to buy the kid a drink. A damn hero. What about Doc? Eddie asked.

Old Doc's lungs gave out.

When?

Sometime in '44, kid. Didn't you hear?

Eddie left an unfinished drink on the bar, put on his coat, and went out in the snow. He didn't know why Christmas meant anything to him anymore. In the years in the Pacific, it had just been another sweating day; maybe they gave you a canned turkey, and the chaplain sang hymns. But Christmas to Eddie was still Yance, the log cabin at the ranch, his mother looking kind of wispy over the woodstove, drawing out a goose that Eddie'd shot. He'd been corresponding with his mother pretty regular, except since Okinawa. It puzzled him why she'd never mentioned anything about Doc.

So late that afternoon, Eddie set out from Green River City to hitch a ride north to Beaver. He got on with a gasoline truck for a few miles; then, in the dusk, the driver had to turn east toward the Indian reservation. Eddie said he'd walk. "Storming like this, you better watch it," the driver said. "You know this country?"

"Yas," Eddie said. "I know it."

By nightfall, the storm had turned into a ground blizzard, wind-whipped snow cutting Eddie's face and blinding him as it lashed across the highway. His blood was thinned out from the Pacific. He had no gloves and just a peecutter-little issue cap and a thin Marine overcoat. He kept leaning into the storm, slogging ahead and feeling his way just to stay on the edge of the highway. Often, he'd think he was hearing a car coming, but it'd only be a different-sounding roar of the wind, howling down some draw. In his misery, Eddie got thinking it would be a strange old world, to let him get through the war only to freeze to death here. Home.

About eight o'clock, Eddie figured, a light began shimmering through the snow; Eddie's face had frozen now, and his feet weren't much good, but he began to run, finally coming onto an old stone building looming up out of the sagebrush. Block letters over the door read "The Morris Hotel." Why in God's name it had been built out in the middle of nowhere, fifty miles from anything, Eddie sure didn't know. In fact, as Eddie recalled, the old Morris had been deserted for years. But now it appeared there'd been a change; the downstairs, where the lobby used to be, had been made into a grocery and mercantile. The place was dark; the light Eddie had seen was just a blue neon Mountain

Dairy Milk sign, burning in the window. Eddie tromped around the big two story building, looking for some sign of life. Out back in the drifting snow, there was an empty garage and an old hay rake. Eddie kept peering at the upstairs windows, the hotel rooms, but they were dark and cold.

There was a gas pump in front of the hotel; Eddie thought he'd pour some, get a fire going and at least thaw. But the gas pump was locked tight. Fumbling with the lock, Eddie realized he'd lost the feeling in his hands. He turned and ran up the steps to the door of the grocery. He drew back to kick the glass in, but at the last moment—for God's sake, there was a light, moving slowly in the dark rear of the store. Eddie began banging on the glass, hollering, rattling at the lock.

Then an overhead light switched on; the wind and snow kicked the door open about three inches until it caught on its latch. A girl was peering around it. "What do you want?"

"Come in . . . ?"

"We're closed . . . "

"Ma'am! I'm freezing to death. Been walking—"

The girl had the strangest color hazel eyes, and now she seemed to size Eddie up and be worried about him. At least her eyes showed that. She pulled him inside, slamming the door. "Come into the back," she said. "I was just studying . . . by the stove."

He followed her down the aisles of the mercantile, and she led him into the old Morris Hotel kitchen, with the smoke-stained walls and the high old Monarch stove. "Stand right there," she said. Eddie backed up to the stove. He was trembling by now, shivering like he had a sudden fever.

"I saw you out there," the girl said. "But I was kind of scared. I'm here alone."

Eddie's teeth were chattering, and, in the relief of being inside, he wanted to cry. Jesus Christ, why cry! But he tried to grin and say, "You . . . don't have to be scared of me."

She was half sitting on the kitchen table, watching him. She had reddish hair with a kind of long face and yet hollowed around the cheekbones and a wide level mouth. She wore a sweater that was angora or something awful soft, and closer up she smelled sweet. What happened? Eddie thought. Because she was holding him by the arms and saying: "You sick? You going to faint?"

Then maybe he did. When he came to he was lying in an upstairs bedroom of the old hotel; there was a light on out in the hall; somehow he remembered crawling in that hall with the girl and her angora tugging at him. The storm was rattling the dark window pane, and Eddie's head ached like the top would blow off. Then there was a little scrape of shoes; a hand touched him on the forehead. It was like ice, started him into another spell of shivering.

The girl said, "I can't get the doctor. The phones are down. And no car either with the folks gone. Your fever's pretty high. We've got to break it." Then she peered closer at him. "Did you get sick in the war? Malaria maybe? Are you hurt someplace?"

Eddie wasn't able to answer. He just lay there creaking the bedsprings; then he got so tired and drifted away. Next thing he felt seemed familiar somehow, burning down his throat. The girl was propping him up, and he could taste the tea she was pouring into him, whiskey, lemon in it too. It seemed to trickle down and warm each bone of his spine. He began to grin and said, "I sure found you at the right time. Do you take care of everybody like this in the old Morris Hotel?"

She must have seen that he was coming back to his senses a bit, for slowly she drew away. "You can drink that yourself now," she said, standing up.

"What are you, some kind of nurse?"

"I'm studying to be one. But I didn't expect to have to practice here. I think you have malaria. From what I've heard about it, you look like you do."

"Ain't you awful young to be a nurse?" Eddie said.

"I'm nineteen. How old are you?"

"About a thousand," Eddie whispered.

Then back it came. The tea inside of him seemed to have cooled now. He reached down to try to pull his Marine coat over him, but just that effort set off another chill. The girl held his head with her ice hand, then ran and returned with a big quilt. It helped for a bit, but the blizzard was drumming the windows and the snow swirling someplace behind Eddie's eyes. Again, he was so awful tired and fading out of sense; but, when he came back, the girl was lying on top of him, hugging him to keep him warm, then rubbing the back of his neck, his arms and chest through the covers. "It's all right," Eddie whispered. "It's better. Thank you . . . " And drifting away again with the girl saying, "I don't know what else to do."

Well, that was her: Sandra Szorgy. Last daughter of an immigrant coal miner from Rock Springs, youngest of seven kids, and the cutest. That's why her pappa Andy called her Doll.

Four days later, her folks came home. Andy and Maria Szorgy were hard-bitten old country people, Andy with a leather cap and Maria with her head wrapped in a black shawl. When Andy quit the mines, he'd used his disability money to start buying the old hotel, set up a mercantile for the few farmers and ranchers out in middesert. Hoped someday—now the war was over—there'd be tourists passing through. But the tourists would pass through and keep going, that was the trouble with the hotel. Andy was almost broke. In fact, he'd made the trip to Rock Springs to stall off the mortgage holder. Andy, the spring before, had even started to hand-dig graves to keep the family going. Wages were five dollars a grave.

On the morning Eddie had recovered—and it was a malaria attack, the doctor said—they gathered in the upstairs parlor, Eddie, Doll, and her folks. The storm had blown out now and the long fields of the middesert country were crusted with diamond-shaved snow. "Eddie's people have a ranch," Doll said. "Little place up by Beaver. He wants me to go there with him. Get married." Doll had been looking out the window; she stood so erect in her dark gray dress; she had a green scarf stuffed into the throat, and now when she turned to confront her parents, the scarf was the same fierce color as her eyes.

"Ahhhh, Dollie," Maria Szorgy sobbed.

Andy Szorgy banged his fist on the potbellied stove. "Gotdam! You know the man four days. What you mean, fella, coming in here like dis? You some tramp? My Doll is no tramp!"

Eddie stared down at the rough leather of his Marine Corps combat shoes. "If it was just four days, it was like a lifetime to me."

Maria wailed now, with Doll trying to comfort her. And Andy clumped downstairs. "Jesus Christ, I get drunk on dis one!"

For nearly two weeks, Eddie stayed in the old hotel while Doll wrangled with her family. Eddie was plumb miserable, weak from malaria and the yearning for Doll, too. The old lady watched her like a damn prison guard; but still in the night Doll managed to tiptoe down to him. And then Eddie was worrying because, hell, it just wasn't practical, him with no job, not knowing what had happened at the ranch; didn't even have a secondhand truck to take the girl away in. And also, it seemed sensible to find out about Doll; have her around at saloons and dances, watch her in action; maybe she'd turn out to be some whore who'd been down with everybody in the country.

But no, not Doll. Eddie was sure of this. They were starting fresh and joyous, too. They'd go scrambling out in the snow, she pelting him with snowballs and he scrubbing her face, playing like the kid Eddie hadn't been for so long now. Finally, even old Maria gave in and let her daughter go up to the ranch with Eddie, see what she was getting into. Eddie by now had the loan of a truck from a miner friend of Andy's. He and Doll started up the eighty miles toward the mountains and Beaver. The sagebrush tops were poking yellow through the snow; it was a warm and peaceful pale sky. Eddie driving slow, with Doll's head on his shoulder, telling her how proud he was going to be to show her old Yance's place, meet his mother too. And they got to dreaming then . . . well, Eddie could build the ranch up, get enough cattle to pay for groceries, then maybe go into that resort business, hunting and fishing parties like old Doc was talking of. Most of all, there'd just be times of Doll and Eddie alone, back out in the big basin, making love as unashamed and free as does and bucks.

It was late afternoon when they got to Galusha's turnoff, where the road quit. Eddie hadn't thought to borrow snow-shoes when they passed through Beaver, didn't really want to waste time stopping. But to his surprise, off along the edge of Moon Creek and up through the timber there was a pretty good trail, signs of snowshoes and a team and sleigh both. On the packed snow, Eddie led Doll up into the valley. She ran some of it until her face got wet with snow and red huffing. She was giggling, sliding her hands into his pants pockets to warm them. "In just a minute or two," Eddie said, "we'll bust out of the timber, and you can see it."

The sun had gone down now; it was just blacks and browns and the silver of the deep snow, but, to Eddie, it looked like a picture on a Christmas card, the main log house with a good two feet of snow on the roof; then, the big drifts curling up around the log barn and the corrals. But out in the meadows in the stackyards, the fences were down, and there wasn't any hay. That puzzled Eddie, how his mamma could get along without hay for the team. Also bothered him why, on as cold a day as this, there wasn't smoke coming out of the chimney.

"Oh my God," Doll said, "it's beautiful. I never knew it was like this up here."

"You just seen the beginning of it," Eddie said. They hugged for a minute, looking down on the old place; then Doll said, Race you there. She begin to run, long-legged and lithe as a deer. Hell, Eddie was too tired and still a little weak to fight that deep snow. He let Doll beat him to the cabin porch as he slogged past the corrals, looking at so many memories.

"Eddie?"

Doll was standing on the porch, back to him; there was no laugh in her voice now. He ran up beside her, and he saw the open creaking door, with snow drifting into the parlor. "Jesus Christ!" Eddie cried. "Mamma!"

"She can't be here," Doll said. "There's nobody here."

Eddie burst inside. There were rabbit pellets on snow that was covering most of the floor. A couple of pillows on the old red sofa were torn open. Eddie swung from one wall to the next. Yance's belongings: the pictures, Indian war lances, the traps. The walls were bare, one old picture hanging half loose like it had been pulled down. "Them sons-of-bitches!" Eddie cried. "They've robbed the place."

He ran across the parlor into the kitchen; the pots were all gone, cupboards open and stripped; from there, he ran stooping down into the first bedroom, then into the little room beyond. Bedframes still there, mattresses, but all the bureau drawers had been emptied, the contents showered on the floor, whatever of value Eddie was sure had been taken. He came back into the parlor, and, when he found even old Yance's branding irons were missing from beside the chimney, it was like a lead fist striking Eddie in the throat.

"Well by God," he cried, "I'm gonna catch them, whoever done this—" Then he glanced over at Doll, who was hugging her arms around her breast in the freezing cold, sniffling.

"It's too damn bad about you, honey," he said, "starting with this mess. But we'll get it straight."

Her lip trembled. "We can't even stay here tonight, can we?"

"We damn well are," Eddie said. "Start a fire, rustle up something."

"But hadn't we better go to town, find out about your mamma?"

Eddie frowned at Doll; she sure acted scared and wanting to get out bad. "We ain't going no place," Eddie muttered. And that prediction, unfortunately, was one of the truest he ever made.

By the time they'd gotten the snow swept out and a fire started, a light snow had begun falling outside. Later, as Eddie walked to the corral and split some wood, the flakes were big and heavy. He wondered then about trying to get out, but he was too damn mad; he wanted to root in and get the place livable. But all Doll could find in the cupboards was one can of peaches, flour, and baking powder.

Well, they stretched the biscuits and peaches two whole days, while outside a ground blizzard whipped up around the cabin eaves, and the whole world went quiet and white. Hell, Eddie didn't even have a gun to shoot a rabbit with, if he could have seen one in the storm, which was unlikely. And a few times in those two shivering days, Doll did break down and sob. Was this really what living here meant? So lonely, no phone, no nothing. She'd been in nurse's school down in Denver, where you could run out in the car, get to a show. But here now, just the two of them, snowed in all the time.

"Yas goddammit," Eddie growled. "If you don't want to stay, now's the time to find out."

That made her cry more, and then Eddie got to hugging her in the cold dark parlor, trying to give her courage to stick with him; they'd make a go of it.

Well, it seemed like Doll did a lot of sobbing that first couple of years. Things were sad indeed when Eddie got 'em all sorted out. His mother had died in a Salt Lake hospital just about the time Eddie had sailed from Okinawa. There'd been mail sent to him by relatives, telling about her death, but hell, with the war over, that mail was probably rotting in some Fleet Post Office depot. And, when Eddie got to Beaver and learned of the death, he also raised hell with the sheriff, as to how if the ranch was in an estate, it hadn't been locked. The sheriff said it was locked; some tramps or out-of- state hunters maybe had busted in there and raised hell.

But Eddie knew better, and so did the editor of the newspaper in Beaver. They were locals who had busted in when they knew Polly was dead and gone. Sure enough, the editor wrote a column about Eddie, this hero, coming home to a looted home. Nothing would be said if the belongings were returned . . . at night to the back porch of the news-paper office. Well, not all came back; but a few of the miserable sneaks that had stolen Yance's old traps and Indian rigs, they did return them under cover of night. But the anger of it left in Eddie a bitterness toward the town and the trashy buggers that hung around the saloons and motels and would rob you of game or any other damn thing if they had a chance.

Maybe, in fact, that was the whole sad struggle of Eddie and Doll's life together. One word: town. It seemed like in the early years, building the ranch back up, Doll worked so damn hard, and at the same time she was having the kids; Junie first, then bing-bang right quick, Ly . . . and thank God a breather of about eight years before Susan came, more or less by accident. And it wasn't that Doll and Eddie didn't love each other dearly: they loved to a passion. But Doll always was a little pouty when night would come, or a weekend, and there'd be no way short of snowshoes, packing babies on their backs, to get out of the ranch, go to town.

Unlike Eddie, Doll needed people, and she was good at bossing people around. Eddie could see that developing in her as the years went on. She used to say to him that she needed a challenge, whatever the hell that meant. And, for a few years, she seemed busy enough, even for her. She was teaching the kids school in the kitchen, by Calvert Correspondence Courses; and she was sewing, baking bread, writing some kind of Red Cross letters for the Korean War; on top of that she'd help Eddie feed the cows and even give him a hand with the colts he was breaking in the deep snow.

But the fall that Junie was starting fifth grade, life out at the ranch, the way Eddie wanted it, came to an end. Junie got sick with an ear infection; they had to rush him a hundred twenty miles to the Green River City hospital, and even then he nearly died. After the smoke settled, the doctor studied Junie and said the boy wasn't in too good shape. Well, Eddie and Doll had known all along that Junie was an awkward disjointed sort of kid, with a terrible temper on him and also screaming fits in the night. The doctor said Junie'd had pretty serious damage to his brain, at birth or in an injury; now, the high fever of the ear infection wasn't going to help. The boy would have to be watched pretty carefully for a time and also given extra lessons in school so he could catch up with his class.

It all came down to the fact that Doll said, "Eddie, we can't raise these kids like wild animals out here anymore. Summers are fine, they can help you and all the rest. But winters, we're going to town. The county will pay us a board bill to live someplace."

"You go right ahead and go," Eddie said.

"But you can get a job on the highway crew, over the winter."

"I got cows to feed."

"Sell 'em, Eddie. You know it's time you sold and went to guiding full time. It's the only way we can come out up there, small as we are."

The damn bitter thing was that Doll had been right. In modern times, old Yance's homestead was just too small and too winterbound to be economic as a ranch. It took Eddie two lonely winters of feeding his damn cows and longing for his family to come to him on the weekends . . . took him that time to finally kick the cows in the butts and ship 'em to auction. Out of the proceeds, Doll bought a little house in town; just for the kids, she said, so Junie could smash around in there playing football, which he loved; seemed like the clumsier he'd get, the stronger he was; hell, he'd run crashing into bigger kids without any fear. Doll said it was again on account of the brain injury: he didn't quite realize the dangers. And Ly . . . Lyman, he was the president of his class and the student council, and he played in the band, did acting, and the like. Susan, of all of 'em, she was the one who'd hop into the truck with Eddie and plow out through the snow to the ranch, feed his horses or get ready to open the place in the spring. After selling the cows, Eddie did spend some time in town, those winters, odd-jobbing, mending harness, or driving a truck; and it seemed like Susan would be sitting on his lap, showing him her new dress, or Ly would come in with a damn tuxedo Doll had rented him for the school prom; and Junie, he'd be out in the garage, taking his beat up truck apart, hammering on it, and putting it back together.

Then, one day, the kids were all gone. Eddie had been busy that fall, hunting: he hadn't expected it. Or truthfully, he hadn't let himself look at it. Junie was off to the service, Ly to the university, and Susan signing herself on at the damn hostess school. By now, too, Doll had been working for Ambrose, the local doctor. Seeing that Ly wanted to have an expensive education, and God knows Eddie didn't earn no real keeping money whanging hunters and fishermen, Doll had gone back and got her nursing degree. The job paid well, and, as she said, it was the challenge she needed. Hell, those women in town, in addition to Doll's job, they had her running this welfare deal or that Girl Scout cookie sale. Eddie couldn't keep up with all the silly things people did in that town. But, then, when he woke up and realized the kids were gone, he got an awful horror that he was going to end up like one of them rocking chair rubes, setting on the main street with nothing to do but think back about the times of being free and young.

It got Eddie so perplexed, in fact, that one noon hour he went and hauled Doll out of the clinic, put her in the truck, and drove her far up into the Shoshone mountains, to a lake. There, Eddie got her out, put his arm around her, and they had a couple of beers and sandwiches in the drowsy sun. And Eddie said, goddammit, he was so lonely now and kind of scared, too, for the first time in his life: he wanted her back with him, the way they'd begun, fixing up the old place, sweeping out the cobwebs and the snow . . .

Poor Doll, she just leaned on his shoulder and bawled. She said how much she'd loved him always, didn't he know? Sure, he knew. It was just that, for twenty-some years the world had kind of pounded them apart; time to go home now, wasn't it? And they did.

Doll changed things around so she could work just a couple of afternoons a week at the clinic. Rest of the time she was puttering, fixing up the old cabin, sewing and writing letters, and whatever else a woman did when she got to be forty-some with her kids gone. Also, she'd go with Eddie on some of his pack trips. She hated camp cooking for a bunch of dudes, but she did it occasionally; then took up painting in watercolors on the long afternoons when Eddie had the dudes out fishing, and she was alone in camp.

They were awfully happy days for Eddie, having Doll back. But he knew, even then, that they couldn't last. The Galushas, the neighbors, had a little piece of land downriver, some distance from Eddie. But, in the spring, they sold it off for tourist cabins and got a damn fortune for a few acres of sagebrush and river. Well, Doll was too much of a business-woman to let that slide by. She got totting up what their place would be worth. Eddie refused to listen to her, but, as she said, she was just sort of dreaming about their old age.

But then they did get old, quick. At least it hit Eddie so hard. Junie's death. Hell, they couldn't even say for sure that he was dead. *Presumed dead.* Missing in action. Nothing left of Junie but a goddamn Silver Star. For what? And Eddie could see, looking at himself in the mirror, the wrinkles cut into his face and his skin turning old. Junie had been all Eddie's kid, the fighter, taking on any odds; and, then, there on the trails in the summer, Junie was the one who'd saddle up, shoe horses, chop wood. The basin was even more Junie's than Eddie's; and many times they talked about how Junie would be running his own dude string soon.

Well, Junie was gone, then Susan was off flying; and of course Ly was out in another life: hell, Ly never gave a second thought to the old ranch. He had his "dental practice." So, as Doll said, "It's getting too hard to fight alone, Eddie. We're at a point where we better think about our future now."

And what scared Eddie the worst was that Doll was like a damn giraffe, her long neck thrust up, always peering ahead, seeing events far off. Trouble was, she'd been right most times in the past. That's what tore at Eddie now that he was about to lose his permit. She had the bug to go to California, and that was just the beginning of the end. Eddie was too lonely here without the kids, and he loved Doll too much to live without her. And yet, to give up the ranch and cut himself off from the only life he'd ever known . . . he knew he couldn't do that either.

Maybe then, it was about like Doll said: could be a blessing if the Game and Fish would lift his permit. At least Eddie wouldn't have to decide it himself. It would kind of be the hand of God, settling the last part of their lives.

CHAPTER 4

"IT'S a great old state," said Claude Eggers, the governor of Wyoming. Claude had on his roughout working cowboy boots, silver belt buckle, string tie; but he'd taken off his Stetson, for it kept bumping the top of the airplane as he peered out the window. Claude was not actually a cowboy; in fact, he'd been a life insurance salesman in the million dollar a year club before he got into politics. But Claude was a big rough fellow; he'd played running guard at the university and been mentioned on several second string All-Americans. He looked like he could have been a cowboy, and, when you were governor of The Cowboy State, you had better look like one.

The legislature was still pretty much dominated by land-owners; the stockgrowers were the political power, and had been since statehood. But now, and with credit to Claude Eggers, the great old state was starting to spread new wings. The man with him in the private jet was R. W. Conant of San Diego, California. To the average sheepherder out in the desert, where the jet circled, the name wouldn't have meant a thing. But on the Big Board, Conant AirTronics was one of the most successful conglomerates, a growth stock that rode up on jet aircraft modifications and space oriented electronics, spurred on by Ronald Reagan's Star Wars project. And, thanks to Ras Conant's wisdom or luck, he had diversified also into profitable small manufacturing lines.

Ras Conant masterminded a multinational empire; yet he was still an open-faced Illinois farm boy with a directness Claude Eggers liked. Oh, to be sure, some of Claude's

65

political opponents said, "you're giving Conant the key to the state treasury." Untrue: Claude's generosity was simply because he saw real value in Conant for Wyoming. Here came a man who was going to reopen and rebuild the old coal town of Garnerville, turn it into a new center of operations for ConAT light manufacturing: kitchenwares, snow machines, boats. What Claude could see, and why he encouraged all state agencies to help Conant, was a payroll of maybe five hundred people and a nicely increased tax base: the first inroad by an aggressive company to build a new industry in the state. Beyond that, Claude suspected Conant might have plans for developing more strip coal out of the old Garnerville slopes and even pioneer into oil shale.

In fact, this was where Ras Conant's jet flew now, over the long yellow ridges of the desert and the scattered reservoirs and creeks turned copper in the late sun. Vast oil shale beds lay under here, Claude explained. Then he beckoned at the state geologist to bring up the maps and show them to Mr. Conant.

But Conant was studying the land below with fieldglasses. He had a big thick face, dark-skinned and heavy wavy hair. Young-acting man, maybe fifty. "Drop your gear and flaps," he barked into the microphone to the pilot of the jet. Then, without turning away from his glasses, he told Claude and the state geologist to forget the maps. He was looking at a big band of antelope out near the reservoir.

"Oh, we could show you more antelope than that," Claude said. "We sure got antelope."

Conant was having the jet circle now and go lower. For a good three or four minutes, he watched the antelope; then ordered the pilot to proceed back to Cheyenne. "With game range like that out in this desert," Conant said, "it'd be a pity to strip it for oil shale."

"Well, I wouldn't let that worry me," Claude chuckled. "We've got millions of acres for our game. We've got plenty of places antelope can go."

Ras Conant lit a long cigar and put his feet up on the jet seat beside the governor. "I'll tell you something," he said. "Our kind of people in our plants, this is what you can't buy for 'em. Get out with a boat, a gun, a fishing rod. Used to be able to do that in California, but the state's a damn tenement now. And the last earthquake tipped the balance. The moving companies won't give you the figures, but we know how many are leaving. So that's why we're here." He sucked the cigar. "Keep that open space to yourself. You got an asset in it."

The lieutenant governor, also in the ConAT jet, leaned forward. He was so damned ingratiating, Claude wished he hadn't brought him. "Speaking of game, Mr. Conant," the lieutenant governor said, "we've heard you're quite a hunter yourself. One time the wife and I were looking at TV, and we saw a show about you—"

"Oh that damn thing," Conant said. Then he chuckled and explained how a network had been bothering him, wanting to have a tour of his den, where he kept his game animals. And, yes it was true, he'd shot just about every kind of trophy in every land.

Conant seemed pleased to be asked about hunting. He mused on, trading stories with the lieutenant governor until Governor Eggers felt slightly upstaged. Then, it struck him. Joline Roush, whom he'd known at high school and played football with. Joline had had a cup of coffee with him in the privacy of his office a few days before.

Claude cleared his throat. "As long as you boys are talking about big game hunting," he said breezily, "I wonder if Mr. Conant has ever shot a moose?"

Conant shrugged, "Oh I got one in Alaska. A fair head, nothing exciting. But your moose here are smaller, I understand."

Claude Eggers smiled. "They're supposed to be."

"What do you mean by that?"

"Mr. Conant, I have just seen a moose that ought to be in

somebody's record book. Yes indeed, a Wyoming moose
. . . " He went on then to explain how one of the game
wardens had stumbled on the animal, brought his picture in.
"You ought to have a look, Mr. Conant. Your mouth will
water."

"It usually does," Conant said. "I hope someday to be
able to hunt in Wyoming. Didn't put in for a permit this
year; too busy getting the plant move straightened out."

Claude Eggers leaned back in the softness of the jet chair.
He really liked Ras Conant. Wyoming needed people like
him. "Well," said Governor Claude Eggers, "I can tell you
. . . like the hundreds of thousands of others who come here
. . . you'd enjoy a hunt in our beautiful fall scenery. And if
that moose appeals to you, Mr. Conant . . . don't worry, we'll
get something arranged."

Ras Conant brightened. "Well now, when does the moose
season open?"

Claude Eggers started to say he wasn't quite sure: he'd
find out when they landed. But the lieutenant governor had
jumped in with both feet. For an ex-sheriff, he was learning
politics quickly. "It opens," he said, "in exactly ten days."

Eddie and Doll got it decided finally that she better go
down to California and have a visit with Susan. It was a good
time to go, before elk hunting season; not that Eddie had
many hunters coming, but he liked Doll to be there to get
supplies, handle the phone, which was always ringing from
somebody's office or other. Doll begged Eddie to come with
her; after all, she said, Susan still needed her pappa too, even
though she was living away. Doll suspected Susan had a
fellow and was thinking of getting married. All the way down
to Green River City in the truck, Doll kept begging Eddie to
change his mind and come on. They stayed in a motel that
night, went to a show, and she kept begging him.

Eddie was torn. It wasn't that he didn't want to see Susan.
He loved that little girl. But he was scared too. If once he

got there, and kind of relaxed, he imagined that he might start thinking that this is the time in his life to go soft, set around in some kind of work like taking tickets in a parking lot, and stare out at the blue Pacific: say, I'm here, my life's work is done.

No, Eddie thought: it was better not to look yet. There might come a time if he was crippled or something he'd have to go. But right now there was too much on his mind, too many chores needing doing before hunters came. By the time Eddie drove Doll to the bus, he'd convinced himself he had to hurry up home, there was so much to do. But when he kissed her good-bye, and she said she'd call as much as she could, when the bus pulled away and went down between the buttes, Eddie felt empty and slow. He was no longer anxious to get back up to the valley.

He stopped at a gas station, had a bottle of beer. Then he dawdled up the highway, seeing what he hadn't seen for a long time. It was the same road that he'd walked that night coming home after the war, but now it had been widened and changed around so much that Eddie couldn't tell just where the blizzard had caught him. The old Morris Hotel had burned down long ago. There was a Chevron station setting where it had been. Around the station were a lot of campers and trailers, some damn caravan of hunters coming into the country. They carried their trail bikes on the front of campers, and some also had jeeps towed behind.

Eddie reflected then on what a lot of the conservation bugs were saying: how all these hunters and fishermen were a great thing for the economy of Wyoming. Why, hell, Eddie thought, them buggers came in like invaders, lugging their own food, whiskey, gasoline, beds. Some of the big caravans had washing machinery with them, that's what Eddie had heard. A few even packed their own doctors, where the doc liked to hunt and fish. So as far as Eddie could tell, they didn't spend a red cent in the country. They just took from it, piled back out the roads with deer, elk, or moose carcasses

strapped on their hoods. Some of the more organized outfits, Eddie knew, had even taken to canning fish; yes, they'd
catch them by the jillions out of the high lakes, stuff them in
cans, and take 'em home.

So Eddie wasn't right happy about this big recreation idea,
where it was enriching the country. It was sure getting to be
competition for him, or any outfitter. There was only so
much game or fish for all to share. On the other hand, he'd
starve like he had before if he went back to cows. No, that
too was out of the question. You just went along, riding
things out, clinging to what you had. This was how Eddie
drove, slow, up to Beaver. He stopped for a second beer at
Cousey's Saloon and finally went on home.

Since that night of coming back after the war, Eddie'd
always had a funny sensation as he approached his home.
He would come through the last swatch of aspen, see the
valley below, and there'd be a real sense of delight: that
there was no place like this in the world. Then, in the next
breath, he'd feel a little chill. The log buildings looked dark
and spooky; like a lightning rod, this place always seemed to
draw down trouble, even violence. Maybe it was just Eddie,
living so far back and seeing so few people . . . but it always
seemed to him when he came home there was bad news lying
in wait. One time, it was a damn good horse, caught himself
in a cattle guard. Another time, the coyotes got Susan's
sheep. Or his neighbor Galusha would be crowding Eddie
again over fencing; or some tourist would be fishing in the
stream and nasty as hell when Eddie put him off.

But this time, no, Eddie drove through the burled aspen
gate and found he was just there alone. The dog hadn't died;
nobody had broke into anything. But he hadn't been home
ten minutes when Joline Roush called. He said he'd like to
come out and see Eddie, had some news for him.

"Good or bad?" Eddie asked.

Joline's voice seemed to tighten. "That depends on you."

After Eddie had hung up and reflected, he was damn sure

the coming home jinx hadn't broke. And when Joline finally arrived and sat there on the porch in the dusk, it seemed Eddie was right.

Joline said that the good part was: remember that moose they'd seen? Well, that moose now had a trophy hunter coming after him, friend of the governor's . . . special deal, what they called a Governor's Permit. Joline himself had been asked by the governor to take this big shot hunting. Joline had explained to the governor that the moose, though in the national forest, was pretty much back in an outfitter's permit; and there was no access to that part exactly except through the outfitter's camp. Well, the governor said, why not get this outfitter, you, Joline, and the hunter together, have a party? Then Joline pointed out that the outfitter's permit had a cloud on it right now; the Game and Fish was probably, for a confessed offense, going to have to take the permit away. The governor however kept going back to the party idea—getting a hunt organized together—and just possibly the outfitter's permit problem, thanks to his cooperation with the state, could be taken care of.

It had taken Joline a good fifteen minutes getting this full story out. He was sitting in the rocker on the cabin porch, creaking back and forth as he talked; then taking long pauses and squinting out at the first bats that were darting around the pines. When he finished, he didn't look at Eddie, just kept creaking.

"They're making a deal, in other words," Eddie said.

"Now, it's not certain that your permit will be cleared, but it sure looks that way. And I guess you know, I've been a friend of Claude Eggers since football days."

Eddie nodded slowly. "It was you who told him about the moose?"

"Yes, I did. Just came out in conversation. Then, later, the hunter entered into it." For the first time, Joline glanced over at Eddie. "Somebody's going to get that moose, Eddie.

You said you didn't have any moose hunters, but he's not going to stay put. He'll ramble."

"He'd be safe back here," Eddie said, "until I wanted him."

Joline nodded, then slapped his hands on his knees and, as if with effort, pushed himself up. It was dark on the porch now. Eddie could no longer see his eyes. "Well, you heard the proposition," Joline said.

"And if I don't happen to go for it?"

"Well, aside from your permit—which is not yet settled either way—I can tell you, Eddie, the governor wants that moose for Mr. Conant. That's the hunter, Conant. So we're going to get that moose. If we have to come through here, we'll come through."

"You will, like hell!"

"Eddie, I doubt you can keep us off National Forest."

"Well, you just watch how quick I can. Hell, you'd go in there, Joline, tromp around after this famous moose. Then the word'd get out that I was letting people back on the permit. Anybody could come through here. Well, that would sure finish my business quick. Is that what your outfit wants? Are you trying to hang me between two horses?"

Joline didn't answer directly. He just said it'd be wise if Eddie thought about it before he made too rash a decision. Then he walked down off the porch and got into the green Game and Fish truck. The lights cut a circle around the log buildings as Joline drove out. Then the place grew dark again and still.

"Goddammit," Eddie whispered to no one, "I am back in the corral again. The sons-of-bitches have put me there, and this time, there ain't no gettin' out."

CHAPTER 5

IT was way back in '74 when Eddie had first felt the bone of it in his throat. Doll and them had started telling him he'd have to choose now how he was going to live. Was it the way he'd been born to—the Big Open, the freedom of it? Or would the city folks and the government finally trap him and tame him and make him into one of them?

By then, Doll had started saying, "It's ended here, Eddie. Not your fault, not anybody's. While you're still young enough and not crippled up, you got to get out and make something of your life."

"Make like hell what?"

"Well, money for one thing," Doll had replied. "Eddie, I love this place, this wilderness, like you do. But outfitting is a dead end now. It's slow starving; two, maybe four months a year is all the time you have to get a paycheck."

She was sure right about that. With everything going up. Inflation, taxes. They hit you on every part you bought, horseshoe, even a bullet, and gasoline the worst of all. "I'm sick," Doll used to say, "of always being in debt, owing everybody, or avoiding their looks on the street when I know my bill with this one or that one is two or three months unpaid."

"If you're talking selling the place again!"

"I'm not. Keep it, sure. But shut her down in winters, get out to where you can make a decent living. Other people do that. They migrate to where the work is, not just rotting out starving here in Beaver County."

"Not me, by damn!"

73

"But you've never tried! What do you think Junie would want you to do? Mourn and die here?"

By now tears were running down her cheeks, and Eddie was choked up too. Junie had only been shot down and missing in action for six months. All they had left of him was his medals, and the loss of him was tugging out after Eddie's heart.

"Think about what's left, Eddie. How to put your life back together. That's what Ly says."

"Ly? How'd he get into this?"

"Because he loves you, like I do. And we're both worried, Eddie. Any medical book will tell you you've got to work grief out of yourself. Attack it, get it behind you."

"Meaning just what bullshit now?"

"Are you going to talk or just be a mule?"

Finally Eddie grunted, talk.

It come down to the fact that they had it all figured out, she and Ly. Lots of good reasons coming together. One, winter just setting in, Eddie had an awful hacking flu that was going around. Two, Ly was down in Tucson, Arizona, finishing his dental training. Basking there in the nice desert sun with the whole area booming, tourist jobs, dude ranches, building new cities of houses. "Ly has a neighbor who can put you on construction, Eddie. Really big money, steady work. He says they've got kids hammering nails who don't know a tenth what you do."

He could stay in the back of a house where Ly and his wife were living. Then, after a month or so, if he liked it, Doll would take a leave from nursing, or do some in Tucson, and spend the winter with him in the sun. "Now what's wrong with that?" she said, "just trying that?"

"I ain't cut out to hammer nails, regardless what they pay!"

Doll's eyes blazed. "Then are you cut out to put your family back together? To heal it?"

"You talking more medical bull? Who you listening to anymore?"

"My heart, Eddie. And what I think is in yours." She gripped his hands. "All poor Junie's life—no point trying to make a secret of it to yourself, Eddie—you doted on that boy. You gave him so much love, trying to make up for his shortcomings—and what was left you gave to Susan—you gave it all, and Ly got left out."

"That ain't true!"

"He thinks it is. He told me just last night on the phone, 'Pop never asks me anything personal. I could be away practicing in Africa for all he cares. And as far as helping me with one dollar, when I need it now to get my degree— yeah, it hurts, Mom.' "

"So what am I supposed to do?" Eddie grunted.

"Spend some time with the boy. Be his father, be proud of him, even if his world and yours are so far apart. And if he needs you—he does now—try to help him, if not in money, just showing him you care."

"I always," Eddie said slowly, "loved all them kids. Figured I'd showed it, but maybe I didn't." His eyes lifted to hers. "If I go, you come down quick. I ain't no A-rab set on livin' alone in a tent!"

She said she would. Missed him already now and was proud of him, too. He was gone in the morning, taking the old Dodge powerwagon and heading south through the snow and onto the deserts, where the people who were making something of themselves lived.

From the first day he hit Tucson, the glaring neon of it, the sprawl of houses and the burned-out desert made his heart groan, longing for the cool green of home, even with the snow on it. But he told himself, This is a business for stickers, I guess—this getting old and mourning—so I will stick.

He hammered his nails, and when they saw that he knew how to work, as north country boys always know, they put him to driving backhoe and putting in septics for the old people's city they were building out in the cactus. Nights, he'd set around with Ly and the wife. They'd look at TV, and sometimes on Saturdays, when Ly wasn't in school, he'd take Eddie out to Old Tucson, where they were making a western movie.

It was kind of comical to Eddie, the powdered-ass dudes he'd watch pulling their guns and pretending to come sweeping into town on horses. But it was always the stunt fellers that did the riding or anything that come to possible danger. Anyhow, last time he and Ly went, Eddie drifted down to where the horse wranglers were, and it felt kind of good to smell sweat-leather again, and fresh horsedung. Then he and Ly would plow back to town again in the traffic and watch another night of TV. Being father and son. By then, though, Eddie was making enough wage to pick up Ly's rent and the purchase of some dental tools for when he was on his own. Ly said he was awful grateful, and would sure pay his pop back for every red cent. Eddie believed that too, seeing Ly now as a plumb capable boy. Though, goddam, to spend a life looking into people's mouths, bringing them pain . . .

Christmas came and went, with Doll there for about six weeks. When she had to go back to the clinic in Beaver—they not able to replace her over the winter—Eddie wanted to go back with her so much he could almost taste it. But she just said, "Oh Eddie, you're turning into such a wonderful new man, you really are. You mean so much now, mainly to yourself. Just please, give it a couple of months more. I'll call you the first minute we get a blade of green grass up home."

"I'll damn well know it before you do," he grunted, and kissed her goodbye.

That very morning, he'd taken off from nail pounding to haul her to the airport—he was driving back alone through downtown because he wanted to stop by the bank when he ran through a stop sign. Nobody around, but suddenly out wheels a Tucson cop car, blinking its top light and riding him over to the curb.

A big, mean-looking cop got out, fellow about Eddie's age. He stood by the back bumper, looking at the Wyoming plate. Then he lazed around to Eddie's window. "A snowbird down from the Cowboy State, hey?"

"Yas. Something like that."

The cop was looking at him real careful. "Gimme your license."

Eddie sighed and did.

"Well, they didn't do your ugly mug any good," the cop said. "But then again, I guess you're lucky to have it at all. Hamburger time, Eddie."

"What the hell you saying, mister?"

The cop bellowed with laughter. "Get out, you ugly son-of-a-bitch. Sarge!" Then the cop wrestled his big arm around Eddie's shoulders. "Goddammit, Eddie, did you forget Westy? You had me in my first firefight, that day at the tomb on Okinawa. Flamethrower. You burned 'em to hamburger . . . "

"Well ain't this the all!" Eddie said. "Westy Furn! I thought you got shot at Shuri castle, somebody said."

"Shot but not dead. They can't kill this old desert rat!"

"And here I thought you was giving me a ticket."

"I'm giving you an invitation, that's what."

They sat in one of the quick-lunch joints for about two hours, the city paying Westy, and Eddie not caring about pay. It felt awful good to Eddie to have a touch of something familiar in a strange land. Even if it was just an old war buddy, long forgotten but never really forgotten.

"It's how things happen," Westy Furn said when they went out and stood by his patrol car. "Blind luck. Here I got a ranch to stock with steers. Begging for an old boy to throw in with me, one I can really trust, and I run into Sarge with his Navy Cross!"

Eddie couldn't quite believe what Furn was leading up to.

Furn was always kind of a smartass operator in the Corps. Now he was saying that a year or so ago, he'd married, second time around, a rich lady from someplace else who'd come out to Tucson for divorce. She'd spotted Westy at a roping contest on his day off, and she was crazy for horses and cowboys. She went crazy for him and bought him a little cow ranch southwest of town, down near the border, where they planned to live. As to the police force, Furn said, hell, he didn't need the job, but he could go out on twenty with a pretty good pension that summer. "So now, Eddie, I'm putting together Mexican steers to graze off the grass the Duchess and I got—I call her Duchess for reasons you ain't gonna know. But what I need is a man to do some hauling and cowboying for me. Somebody who's not scared of Mexico either."

Eddie allowed he'd never been there, but figured it couldn't be any worse than places he had. That evening, meeting the Duchess with Westy—she was a looker in them tight satiny pants—they set the deal. Eddie would draw a thousand, one thousand dollars a month! have the use of Westy's cattle truck, and start hauling up steers. That very night, Eddie went back to Ly's house, had a few drinks too many, and tossed his carpentering apron into the fire.

Ly said though: "How well do you know this fellow, pop? I mean, is it something that can last? There's a lot of sleaze bags down here."

"He's a cop, ain't he," Eddie barked. "Twenty years of it, and the Marine Corps before."

Ly said, well okay, and he guessed it was good that Eddie would be out with livestock again. Keep him happy until he could go back up home.

Eddie had Westy Furn's ranch pretty much to himself, and it wasn't much. Not by Wyoming standards anyhow. Just a big swatch of dry spiky desert, rocks, and every living plant on it stabbing cactus spears into him or tearing his shirt when he rode past.

But he did have a horse at least, though in Wyoming they would have shot the worthless creature for bear bait. Eddie batched in a trailer, beat-up old thing set in a tawny canyon. From the front stoop of it, Eddie could see down the long sweep of mesquite plumb into Old Mexico. And closer, he could see a sagging old adobe by the corrals.

Peludo Ramon lived here, bald, toothless old bugger who'd apparently come to Westy with the place. He and Eddie got to hit it off pretty good. The old man would drink tequila every night, after what few chores he had were done. Then he'd pull out a deck of cards for a poker game.

As for work, there was hardly a trace of it. Eddie would ride fences, cobble a few of 'em up that needed, or kill rattlesnakes when they'd crawl down too close to the big house. This was where Westy and the Duchess were supposed to live, but she was waiting to sell her place in town before they made the full move. And, once or twice on weekends, Westy would come down. He and Eddie would rope or doctor some steers. Westy didn't have but about thirty scraggly humpy Mexican corrientes on the place. "Some cow herd," Eddie said, but Westy told him to wait, that when the market got better up in the states he'd start going in big.

About a month later, it did start. Eddie and Ramon would take the truck, a red bobtail Ford, across the line at the crossing point of San Juan. Then they'd track down sand washes and up rocky hill roads, usually finding a sorry rancho at the end where Furn had made a deal on some steers. The business part was all done by the time Eddie came with the truck. He'd just pull out Furn's Tucson Police card and a fist of Mexican crossing papers. The vaquero at the ranch would whoop the steers into the bobtail. It wouldn't hold but twenty-five of the four-weight kind. Then Eddie and Ramon would creak back up, stop at the Ojos Azules saloon in San Juan for the first cerveza, another one at the border corrals where the Mexican customs bandits got their piece out of it, and the U.S. customs—Smokey-the-Bears, Eddie called 'em, which they didn't like—they got their pound of flesh, too. And finally in the dark, home to the ranch, to dump the steers in the corral, for rebranding the next day.

It was a job that in Wyoming they would have paid you maybe two hundred a month. But Eddie wasn't complaining. It sure beat bending nails. Pretty soon, they'd built up about 125 steers on the ranch. Westy said, "One more load and we'll quit. I'm putting 'em together right now. I'll tell you when."

When turned out to be one afternoon about three p.m.. As Eddie was braiding some roping reins, he heard the rumbles of the Duchess' big yellow Cadillac. Furn was driving it, not in his cop suit though, but wearing dudey western clothes she'd hung on him, even a turquoise bird hanging on a chain around his neck. "Ain't you a candy-ass though," Eddie said, but Furn wasn't in too good a humor about it.

"That last damn bunch of steers," he said. "Told me they'd be ready tomorrow, but they gotta go out tonight."

Eddie squinted up at the sun slipping behind the big blue mountain. "You're gonna run out of tonight," Eddie said, "far as that ranch is and the border and them Smokey-the-Bears closing up. I'll go for 'em in the morning."

"I said, tonight." Furn thrust him the usual fistful of papers, but these had Mexican seals stamped on them. "I've fixed it with the Mexican Aduana and our Customs people. The duty is already paid. They know us, they trust us, and the old Tucson P.D. doesn't hurt."

"No, I imagine not," Eddie said. "What about vetting, though? The federal vet for dipping and inspecting? He's a hard nose and he doesn't hang around long after dark."

"He's at the San Juan corrals right now. I just talked to him. He said it's a little bunch, he could pretty much wave 'em on through. And, knowing us . . . " Then Furn slammed the door and went racing off in the Caddie. Said the Duchess had him going to a big society dinner that night.

Eddie watched the Caddie race back out the dusty road. And felt a little funny notion that he didn't know how long this job was going to last. Maybe part of him was still playing the sergeant, way back when, and Furn, now that he remembered it, had been a smart-off kid whose ass he had to kick a few times.

But once Eddie was on the road with old Ramon, he got over his mad about taking orders from a cop. Ramon was gumming his harmonica, peeping songs that he said were from one of the revolutions he'd fought in.

In the dusk, sure enough as Westy had said, there were cattle being shipped through the San Juan corrals. The vet truck was standing by, and some of the big tractors were creaking out with their pots loaded with bawling corrientes. But hell, it was dark before Eddie got down to the peckerwood starvy old ranch, where he picked up his load, twenty-three real sorry steers, except for one of them who stuck out because he was Charolais crossed with Brahma. He was white as snow and seemed to Eddie, even in the dark, to be so much weightier than the others that he could be starting to bloat. In fact, Eddie had old Ramon ask the vaquero if they got bloat down here. But something must have got lost in the translation, for the vaquero never said either way.

It had to be a good ten p.m. by the time Eddie pulled his load up to the crossing corrals. "Now ain't that hell," Eddie grunted. "I told Furn this place would be shut tight." Sure enough, there wasn't a hide-nor-hair of nobody around.

But old Ramon just chuckled. *"Pase, pase,"* he kept saying, flicking his hand north toward the crossing gate.

Eddie didn't like the smell of it. He had the Mex customs bandits to go through, always wanting a handout, and fifty yards beyond, the U.S. bunch, Customs and Border Patrol cops, always playing bigshot and chowsing drivers.

Ramon reached over and rattled the crossing papers in Eddie's face. "Hey, amigo, ju got factura. Stamp. Done."

"Well, I believe I do at that," Eddie said. And then Ramon got even slyer. The old coyote's eyes gleamed. He scrambled out of the truck and unhitched a gate by the corral. This was where the U.S. cattle trucks backed in to pick up their approved loads. So Eddie just creaked on through the gate, followed where Ramon pointed, out a sand wash, and, in a couple of minutes, hooked onto the highway with all the border nonsense behind him. Eddie figured that in the morning he'd let Furn run the papers down to the powers that were and make it legal, courtesy of the Tucson P.D.

But Eddie felt kind of tired and old, by the time he pulled up the long road into the ranch. Even for a thousand a month, popping truck gears wasn't exactly what Eddie figured was making something of himself.

He crunched the truck into the loading chute. Ramon had already scrambled out and lifted the tail gate, and Eddie felt the steers swaying the truck as they rattled down into the one big corral. Then he heard old Ramon swearing in Spanish and he got out to see why.

Where was the one Charolais cross steer that didn't get out of the truck. He lay there like a mound of snow, stone dead, snot running out of his nose. "I told you he was bloating," Eddie said.

Ramon just shrugged and said, Put him in the dump, no? So Eddie backed the truck through the corral, opened the gate on the far side. He and Ramon rasseled the heavy carcass out until it slid down the side of a steep arroyo here that somebody had been using since God knows when as the ranch dump. When the dead steer slid down through it, he clanged and clinked through old rusty cans and bottles, came to rest in the bottom, waiting for the coyotes and buzzards to pick him clean in a few days.

Eddie trudged up to his trailer and went to bed. But his belly had been bothering him that day, kind of a sour in his throat ever since Furn had come barging out there with his Caddie and turquoise bird. So Eddie was sleeping so light and restless that sometime in the dark the sound came to him. A rattling of tin.

He sat up in his cot. The dump it was! Some critter down in the dump, rattling the old tin cans. Well what? he wondered. Lion maybe? There was a few around. Lion going in after that fresh steer carcass.

Eddie pulled on his boots and slipped out in the darkness. Damn, he wished he had a gun of some kind. He'd always wanted to bag a lion, of which there wasn't none in Beaver. Taxiderm the hide and bring it back to Doll as a coming-home gift.

But he'd barely sneaked through the upper gate of the corral when he heard a grunt of something that wasn't a lion. Not sure, Eddie looked out and saw a little flick of light starting and snapping off in the arroyo. So Eddie moved real quiet now, around the inside of the corral fence. The steers in there were smelling him and growing restless. So he eased up next to the bobtail truck, which was still where he'd left it, blocking the gate to the arroyo. Then he crawled around the truck rear tires and looked down into the arroyo.

The first thing he saw was blood. Black as ink in a little stab of the flashlight. A man in shirtsleeves was squatting there, cutting the gut out of the dead steer. Eddie almost bellowed at him, but when the flashlight snapped on again, he saw on the back of the man's belt a snub-nosed little revolver in a holster. Then the man turned. His arms were bloody and in his fist was a long knife.

He was laughing, lifting his face up to the light now, the light held by old Ramon. And another tough-looking hombre, maybe half-Mex, grinning as he squatted beside the steer.

The man with the knife had just pulled a white sausage out of the steer's bloody intestines. Looked like a sausage, about ten inches long, until Eddie could see that it was wrapped in plastic. The man with the knife was carefully peeling the plastic off until he had just the white sausage itself laying over his palm. Like he was hefting the weight of it, and stroking it. The son-of-a-bitch with the knife was Westy Furn.

Eddie crouched there, not knowing what he was seeing, and unable to believe it either, because it sure didn't fit with nothing good. The tough-looking customer was laughing aloud now, until Furn whipped him a look and put his finger to his lips. Then they began clanking through the cans and up the arroyo side toward Eddie.

Good Christ! Eddie thought, what if they find me here? But his body was answering before his head did, scrunching him around under the truck—not much of a hiding place, just the rear duals to screen him. He could even see Furn's big dudey boots coming through the gate.

Furn screamed. All happened so fast, Eddie never heard the blast, Furn spinning down and the whole damn arroyo chattering and exploding. Eddie smelled it before he knew what it was. Powder smoke. And the rattling-cutting chatter, knew that, too. Machine gun! Oh, not the old kind. Something automatic that rattled off, new way of dying like what they used in Vietnam. Ramon was screaming, and there was a body rolling back into the arroyo.

But no flashes. No lights at all. Eddie could make out several dark shapes. One of them had a black shirt, open at the throat. He caught a glimpse of an automatic weapon in the man's hand. Then another shape was scrambling up out of the arroyo. He was shouting in Spanish, and the words like to slap Eddie across the face, crouching by the tire. *"Otro!"* the man cried. *"Con el truque. El trailer. Arriba!"*

All Eddie really got was trailer. Good enough. They were looking for him now. He heard them slipping away, one of the buggers easing through the corral, others moving along the edge of the arroyo so they could hit the trailer from the backside.

Well you bastards, Eddie thought, you ain't gonna find

nobody home. At first he figured, ease up into the truck cab, fire her off, bust out of here fast, up the road. But the chances are, they had a car out there too, and as slick as these hombres were, they could outrun him before he hit the first house, ten miles north of the ranch.

So Eddie shook his head. No, not running. But the one thing he did know better than them was the old earth. The land and the Big Open of it. Even in this miserable desert, he'd learned every cut, every wash, and where the rocks swallowed you up into the deep canyons.

He saw a light flash, up by the trailer. Last chance now. He slid out from under the truck tires, and down into the arroyo. But not through the canyons. There was a horse track he'd ridden enough times, took that, and where it hit the little connecting wash cutting off left, overgrown with mesquites, he burrowed through them. Yas, they'd find tracks in there if they came with a light. But the wash led into slide rock where even a moose couldn't make a print.

Once Eddie had hit the rock, he knew he had them. They were shouting back at the corrals. Then sure enough, they had a car stashed out, and were wheeling it around, sweeping the place with their lights. Come on up, you bastards, Eddie whispered. And he kept running up the slope, darting from rock to rock. Crawled and dragged himself up all the way until he struck the big saddle on top of the canyon. A lion couldn't have tracked him here.

But Eddie didn't let it go at that. He walked most of the night, down a trail he'd taken once a-horseback, looking for one of Furn's damn stray steers. The trail led into the Papago Indian reservation, and it was along about sunup that Eddie came into an Indian town there. Brush huts, with camp dogs growling at him.

The way Eddie's luck was working though, now, an Indian cop lived in the town. He was just firing up his reservation patrol car when Eddie came up to the window. Eddie wasn't even sure the cop could understand English. But hell, he was just a kid. He grinned and said, "What's on your mind, Mac?" And that was familiar too. Eddie like to blubbered when the kid told him he'd learned "Mac" in the Marine Corps. He'd served in 'Nam.

When Eddie went back to Furn's ranch about noon that day, it was with two carloads of cops, and two more cars standing there by the corrals. But these weren't Tucson P.D., they were Feds. Plainclothes, drug agents. They already had Furn's body in a black plastic bag. Eddie just had to identify him. Eddie found what was left of Ramon by the dead steer in the dump. The old man's cards they used to play poker with were blowing away now down the arroyo.

But it wasn't done. The feds had to haul Eddie up to Tucson, tell his story to a federal judge. "For Christ's sake," Eddie said. "I ain't had nothing to do with this!"

They just nodded and acted like they didn't believe him. Question after question. Did he realize that Furn had had him haul up the other steers as a cover? "Cover for what?" Eddie said.

He knew damn well what, they told him. But after he sat there a couple of hours, shaking his head, telling them to call Doll up in Beaver—they'd already done that, and his neighbors the Galushas, and Ly, and practically everybody except the president of the U.S.—then finally they said, Well, here's what it was.

Furn had rotted out as a cop. Thrown in with some drug runner in Tucson. That was the half-Mexican killed with him. But what Furn didn't know was that the bigger boys had got wind of his shipment. One sausage in that steer's gut worth hundreds of thousands of dollars of Mexican brown heroin. It was the beginning of a big business, which the bigs didn't want to tolerate, cutting in on their territory. So they blew old Westy out of it, and damn near Eddie too.

"How did you know?" Eddie asked. "About them syndicate fellers?"

The agents just nodded and said, We knew.

"So they're going to jail, them rotten buggers?"

The agents just said, Someday.

Then, after hours of it, they hauled Eddie into the chambers of the federal judge, and he had to tell his side of it all over again. Even had to say about Beaver, his outfitting on the homestead, and how he made an honest living up there.

The judge looked up and said, "So why are you down here?"

Eddie just shook his head. "Beats the hell out of me. Makin' something of myself, the wife says."

Then the judge smiled. "You were used, Mr. Bulwer. Officer Furn made you into a mule. I'd advise you to pick your friends better next time. Now, get out of here and get back to where you come from."

"You open that jailhouse door," Eddie answered, "and you ain't seeing nothing but my tracks. And hey, thanks, mister."

Eddie took the powerwagon on up the road that night. Never to leave home again, trying to be what he wasn't. Nobody's mule except his own, from then on.

CHAPTER 6

ON the opening day of moose season, Eddie full expected to have the Game and Fish trucks drive up his road. They hadn't said a word to him or he to them since Joline stopped by. But by midmorning, nobody had showed up, and that made Eddie even more suspicious. Could be, he thought, they'd gone way around west and started in that timber road, the same one the city trash had used.

Speaking of them, Eddie had never even got so much as a call from the sheriff. Of course, Eddie wasn't sitting up nights waiting to have Pankey Briles find a bunch of longhairs when he couldn't find his butt with both hands. Still and all, it offended Eddie that the damn buggers could have got clean away with stomping him. And now that *they* knew how to get into Grubbing Hoe, back in some marijuana den of some city this winter they'd be telling others in their tribe. And the next summer more'd be coming. Hell, maybe they never had left. Maybe they were still back in the basin.

It was thoughts along this line that soured Eddie's stomach, got him to stalking around the lonely cabin, wondering if he ought to start taxiderming a good brown trout he got that summer; then, too, Doll had laid out some carpentering for him. Oh, he had things to do. But, finally, it busted on him that he couldn't stay around the place that day, not if Joline and them were going after that moose. It wasn't exactly a decision, but Eddie made a sandwich, then saddled Lester and took off in the bright fall sun of noon.

After Eddie had ridden an hour or so and Lester was sweating, low scudding clouds ran in over the sun; there was a wind too, coming out of the north. The beautiful world of the basin went dead with browns and grays and the first shuddering of fall. Eddie pulled out a poncho and put it on, for now fine spraying rain was striking him. Well, it was getting to be that time of year, he thought; and he wondered what this ride of his was all about, other than to sashay through the basin hoping to find Joline, or hoping not to find him, he didn't know which.

As to the moose, Eddie wondered about him too. Did the poor dumb brute have any idea that on his horns now pretty much hung a man's livelihood; and more than this, a man's principles? If Eddie'd give in to Joline, let him prowl through with hunters, it wouldn't be long before everybody'd be doing it. What Yance had built up here, what Eddie had nurtured, this sanctuary for game—it'd soon be chewed and ragged away. And with it, finally, Eddie too: sitting out somewhere taking tickets in a parking lot overlooking the Pacific. He didn't know why that parking lot idea stuck in his mind, except it seemed like it was all he'd be good for.

Yet here, riding up the sweet-smelling trail in the lodgepoles, this was a land he still knew, and slowly, the wet quiet of the big timber closed over him. He realized he'd wandered off the trail, but wasn't worried about it. He dismounted and led Lester across a few blowdowns. Occasionally, through the tops of the lodgepoles if he looked up, he could see the distant gray spines above Grubbing Hoe. In the low raggy clouds, there was a skiff of snow on the Spines. That would start the game moving.

Now Eddie thought: but where am *I* moving, just walking here through the deadfalls? Am I going toward that long valley where the timber road would let Joline and them in? No, he thought, I am going sort of parallel to where that road would be. But I am in a completely new part of this timber, something I have not seen before in all my life. And what is bringing me here?

He didn't get the question answered, for then, ahead, he

began to see light at the edge of the timber. It appeared to be a park, a sort of meadow; there were still wildflowers in it, but they were frozen brown and curled; around the edge of the meadow was a fringe of tiny aspen, some no bigger than bushes. They were golden now, and, in the wind and fine rain, they danced like a line of harem girls—what Eddie imagined anyhow as harem girls—bending their knees to one side and swishing their hair. It was a beautiful sight to Eddie, the private dance hall of that little meadow. He sat down beside a lodgepole where the rain didn't drip down his neck, lit a cigarette, and mused on the beauty of this new place, and how, not thinking, just going with the country, had led him here.

A snort from Lester interrupted what reverie there was. The horse pulled back on his rein; Eddie cussed him, and then saw. At the far end of the meadow, on the fringe of the aspen and standing erect was a bear. The sight of it startled Eddie just as much as Lester; but soon Eddie smiled and stood up too so the bear could get an idea of what she was smelling. The bear was a brown, very likely a female about two years old. When Eddie's scent struck her pig face and squinting eyes, she gave a snort that echoed in the timber and boomed all the way to Eddie who must have been fifty feet from her. Then she dropped to all fours; Eddie was sure she was shaking her head as if saying: by God, one of them stinking human things back here! And so she went clumping off through the aspen, mashing the little bushlike trees down with her paws in her hurry to be gone.

Eddie chuckled at her; then, wanting to see where she'd run to—maybe a den she was building for winter—he grabbed Lester and set off after her. Again, this wasn't any route he'd planned; he just went stumbling on into timber on the other side of the meadow, followed it down a slope. Here, the timber played out and sagebrush took over, rolling in gentle hills, the swales of which were rusty and yellow with dying elk weed and fall turning willows. Looking across them, Eddie saw why he'd come. Maybe it was instinct, when a man didn't strive and worry and try to decide—that's when he stumbled onto what he was really looking for.

Out in a pocket of willows, along a tiny creek, Eddie had spotted something dark, figuring first it was the brown bear sow. But no. It was a cow moose and her calf. They hadn't seen or winded Eddie. It looked like the cow was showing her calf how to eat willows, get him ready for winter. She'd bite a leafy willow branch down at the root, then jerk her head to the side. The branch would tear through her teeth with a sound like a rope snapping taut, and then the branch would whip out of her mouth with every leaf stripped. After watching her, the calf quit zipping the branches and just began nibbling leaves straight. It was while Eddie was watching this process that the willows began moving beyond where the cow and calf were. Eddie heard a boggy sucking of mud, and up out of a waterhole came that enormous hatrack and, under it, the black face and Roman nose of the big moose. Moreover, he must have seen Eddie and Lester on the ridgeline, for he was looking directly at them. Having stumbled on the moose like this in all the thousands of acres where he might have been, Eddie knew was more than blind luck; it was kind of an omen, and it seemed to tell him clearly what he was supposed to do. Yas, right now he was supposed to take that bull and put him out where neither Joline nor any Governor's Permit hunter could ever get him. That wasn't exactly saying "no" to Joline, which would result in their lifting Eddie's permit. On the other hand, it wasn't saying "yes" to him either. Eddie would just pretend not to be looking when Joline and them sneaked in the timber road. And after a few days of hunting that miserable country back toward Arapahoe Sink, and finding nothing, Joline and his fancy hunter would be more than ready to quit.

So you, Mister Trophy Bull, Eddie smiled—you're going to do some traveling to a new home. Slowly, Eddie's gaze lifted to the long slope that ran up the east face of the

Spines. In this area, because of its inaccessibility, was some of the last virgin timber in the basin. At the bottom of the east slope were jungles of blowdowns that Eddie had fought through only once in his life and vowed never again. Above, the sidehill was steep and so densely timbered you could never glass an animal in there. And the crest was a sheer cliff against the Spines that no moose or man could climb up or down. You might say, Eddie thought, the place amounted to a great big green deep-freeze. Mister Bull, he said to himself, you're going on ice.

Eddie edged Lester slowly down the slope toward the cow and calf. "Now don't *you* start," Eddie whispered. For he felt Lester tightening up through the withers and dogging his footsteps with reluctance. Eddie passed a dead willow and snapped off a thick branch, then rotated that out toward Lester's eye. Lester began to pick up his feet a little better but still snorted, and his withers were tight in fear as Eddie whupped him in closer.

The cow and calf were standing rigid, watching Eddie's approach. The big bull, protectively, had edged toward them. Now, Eddie thought, would be a good time to have a rifle and fire about two shots in that soft mud in front of them.

"Yaaaahhhhh!" Eddie shouted with suddenness.

The reddish young calf moose gave a pitch and leaped out of the willows. The mother lowered her head, and, for a moment, Eddie thought she'd charge him. But by now Eddie had his rope off the saddle and was whirling it around his head and howling. The mother pawed just once and turned to join the calf on a rapid trot up through the willows to higher ground. Only the big bull stayed now, stood frozen with his tongue protruding between his teeth until Eddie rode to within about fifteen feet of him. And that was as close as Lester would go. With a squeal, Lester half whirled and reared, Eddie cussing him and clinging on for dear life. At the same time, he saw the bull take a lunge forward, throw his giant rack of horns in anger, then slice by Eddie with a heavy grunt coming from his belly. All this took just a flash instant, after which Eddie had all four of Lester's feet again on the ground, and sat breathing hard, watching the bull pursue the cow and calf up to a crest in the sagebrush.

They were moving about ninety degrees away from the direction Eddie wanted them to go, so now he whacked Lester in the ribs and took off on the canter, Lester leaping the big sagebrush and ducking around badger holes, stiff-legging like some old fussbudget. Well, Eddie was glad Lester was watching the holes, for Eddie had his eyes only on the three moose, and now that they'd got the idea it was a horse race, they took out quick.

The big bull led them, never once breaking stride, flinging his hooves up in a magnificent trot that seemed to lift him over the tops of the sagebrush, which was a good two and half feet high. Here came Lester, jumping the sagebrush, ducking and laboring at a canter, but that big bull, he just cruised away, soaring black and crashing through willows, spraying into creeks, his long wattle switching back and forth, his rack weaving and darting through patches of aspen and hardly ever touching a branch. The cow and calf couldn't move as fast; in fact, it got so Eddie on the gallop was paralleling them. But they sure knew that the bull was leading, and they followed.

It might have been two or three miles that Eddie ran them all in more or less open sagebrush and patchy aspen until finally Lester was panting and played out. Eddie reined him in and watched the bull plunge into the massive old lodgepole at the bottom of the slope. The cow and calf had swung over another little rise, but Eddie knew they'd soon end up with the old man.

But still it wasn't good enough, Eddie knew. He wanted to push them back into the blowdown area; there was untouched grass in here, bogs, and springs; once that bull found it, Eddie doubted if he'd leave the country, provided there were enough females; and Eddie might just chouse some more cows in to him. So Eddie kicked Lester off and entered the dark old timber, following the trail the moose had taken. For a time he could hear the big bull crashing on ahead; but then presently the sounds were gone, and Eddie was alone.

By now Eddie was walking, trying to walk, through the blowdowns; damn, it was a terrible place; big old trees tall as his chest lying flat, others burned into great heaps of ashes. Everywhere was the smell of decay and chill darkness now, too. It struck Eddie then that by God he'd got so fascinated chousing that bull, and before that drifting with the lay of the country, that the sun had gone down on him.

Well hell, he thought, he could ride back home. It was only six or seven miles. But now even in the denseness of the blowdowns, Eddie could hear the faint rumbling of thunder. The rain was worsening. Somehow a long wet ride back in the dark didn't appeal to Eddie. Back to an empty house, Doll gone and maybe Joline barging in with the governor's hunter, pressuring Eddie. Considering, it would be a helluva lot better for Eddie to stay out that night, just get lost. He might even give the bull another nudge up the slope in the morning for good measure before he went home.

It didn't bother Eddie that he had no sleeping bag and precious little else. He had an axe, always carried that. He found a blowdown where there were five or six smaller trees. He took to whacking off their wet branches, then shaving some chips off old decayed trunks, down deep inside where they were still dry. Pretty quick he got the branches laid over like a roof and a small fire started. He did have a saddlebag that had some coffee, along with the sandwich, maybe even a forgotten candy bar. Eddie lay his axe down and turned from the warming of the fire.

"Hello! Oh God, I'm glad to see you!"

Eddie jumped a yard. It was a female voice someplace

beyond the pile of limbs he'd been chopping. It had got plumb dark now; Eddie was squinting and finally saw a shape moving around the end of the dead trees. The firelight lit up a pale face and long hair and glow on a rubbery slicker.

"Here," the girl cried; she'd turned away from Eddie and was hollering back in the direction she'd come. "Over here, Benny. I found somebody. Keep walking. You'll be able to see the fire." Then the girl ran toward Eddie and pulled up next to him, blowing into her hands, then rubbing herself in the cold. "We heard you," she said, out of breath. "Heard you chopping this wood, I guess. I just prayed it'd be somebody. Benny's pretty bad."

"What are you talking about?" Eddie said.

"My friend, we been camping together. He got a bad cut in his foot, maybe even broke it trying to climb that mountain up there. I've been trying to get him out since yesterday." Then she glanced past Eddie. "Oh, Benny," she cried. "Good. You're doing better."

Another girl had now come dragging in around the end of the timbers. Long black hair down to the shoulders, kind of a bony face and droopy eyes. Eddie thought: if that ain't the ugliest female! Then, sheepish, it struck him of course that it was a man, this Benny.

The young man dumped down in a heap and grunted, "Oh yeah. I'm in great shape. Let me know when you want to climb some more mountains." Then he added, his eyelids drifting up to indicate Eddie, "Who's this?"

The girl seemed a little embarrassed the way her partner was speaking, for she said to Eddie, "I guess you live around here, don't you?" She went on to say her name was Vicky something or other.

Eddie was so startled to see people out here he didn't register much at first. And the Benny one wasn't paying attention to anything but pulling off his boot and sticking his foot up next to the fire. Then he began to howl and grip his calf just below the knee with both hands, rocking back and forth. "Oh Benny," the girl said. Then, to Eddie: "We got to get him to a doctor. Can we?"

"It ain't like there's one right next door," Eddie said, annoyed. Then he squatted. "Now lemme look at it." He slowly took hold of the Benny one's leg. The bugger's long hair was hanging down dripping rainwater, his mouth drooping, and Eddie could smell the unwashed stink of him. In the firelight Eddie could see a cut just above the ankle, but not deep. Then, too, there was a bruise up under the knee on the shin. Eddie passed his fingers over it gently.

"Yow!" The foot pulled away.

"Goddammit! I ain't hurting you that much. Set still." Then Eddie looked up into the mournful hangdog eyes on the kid and grinned. "What do you think I'm doing? Getting even?"

"Huh?" the kid said.

Eddie stood up slowly and looked at the girl. "I remember you now. That day I came into my camp and found the lot of you. You was fussing around drying off from swimming and piling your hair on top of your head. If I recall, you told me about them little maps the Forest Service gave you."

"Oh God," the girl said. "I'd hoped it wasn't you when I heard the chopping. Look, I didn't have any part of those guys beating you up that day. We were all sort of silly. That was a bum trip, that bunch. Losers, downers. They were stoned most of the time. And don't blame Benny either because he wasn't even there. He came later."

The Benny one looked up. "This is the guy with the camp where we—?"

"Where you was still staying, huh?" Eddie said.

"Please," the girl said, "I can explain everything. I was with that lousy bunch, yes, but they're all gone now. It was just later, after Benny came out from Philadelphia, he wanted to climb something, and I didn't think it'd hurt to go back in to your camp. It was so beautiful up there. You will help us, won't you? Get us to a doctor?"

Eddie hissed a long breath through his teeth. "You don't need no doc," he said to the hangdog kid. "You got a small cut on your ankle and a bruise on your goddamn shin. Tomorrow, I'll put you on the horse, you can ride out if you're in such pain."

"Tomorrow . . . ?"

"Yas," Eddie grunted. "Now set down in here and get out of the storm. We're staying the night."

The kid's nose wrinkled up. "Lying out here all night?"

"You have probably lied in worse places," Eddie said, "and damn sure with rottener companions." Then Eddie turned and hunked back under the lean-to. The girl had kind of a little grin in her eyes. She looked down at the Benny one and said, "Oh come on. It'll be fun." Then she stooped over and crawled in beside Eddie. Eventually, of course, he ended up giving her his poncho to sit on, and put Benny down on Lester's saddle blanket, so his precious butt wouldn't get wet. That's how, with the crackling of the fire, they had what supper there was: two apples, one Hershey bar, and one beef sandwich. The girl, sitting next to Eddie, shivered from time to time. She looked like a pale and drowned little rabbit; rainwater would run to the tip of her perky nose, and she'd shake it off. But she laughed a lot, too, with her shivering and said it was fun being there, and being safe. She reminded Eddie in a way of Susan. They'd be almost the same age.

Eddie had learned at Bougainville and other places how to sleep out and stay warm. In the jungle, he used to rig up pandanus leaves above his poncho and old pulpy leaves and rotten wood below it for softness. But here tonight in the surprise of his visitors and the distance he'd ridden, Eddie was plumb tired, and, when he lay down cramped against the two kids, he didn't pay much attention to water or a tree root under his leg; he just socked off quick and heavy.

Then, for some reason he didn't know—God knows he

didn't have a full belly—he began nightmaring. The first
wild scenes were about Doll and his having malaria, lying
shivering down in the old Morris Hotel. Then it was warm
and springtime, wildflowers popping up, and the sage smelling like rainshowers and perfume. It seemed like there was a
visitor came up to the ranch that May morning, introduced
himself to Eddie; then, by God, Eddie had his arm around
him. It was, of all people, the Lieutenant Whatchamacallit
from Okinawa. No other one. The lieutenant who had sent
Eddie into that tomb. But now, apparently, he'd signed up
to go hunting with Eddie, for he was all excited. He said,
"Eddie, I followed one bear into a hole, back up in the basin.
I think there's likely to be more there, and I'm frightened of
'em. Would you go take care of 'em for me?"

"Well sure," Eddie went. The den was a miserable sort of
cave dug out of the base of a big lodgepole, that is, down
under the roots. Eddie took his service .45 in one hand and
a flashlight in the other and went in head first, groping until
he touched hair. Whatever that bear was, it was dead; the
lieutenant hunter had shot it. Then Eddie crowded his face
in so he could see over the back of the dead sow, and beyond
were two yearlings. One of them lashed out at Eddie, struck
his arm. Before Eddie knew it, he was shooting, the cave
blamming with sound and smoke. Then Eddie came up
coughing, backing out with his gun hot in his hand, and
there were bears yelping under the earth, and Eddie crying
above with the lieutenant hugging him. Eddie said right
then, "My boy Junie is dead, I know he's dead, killed in one
of your goddamn wars."

Then Eddie had forgot the dead bears; he was running
screaming down the trail, crying out for Doll, to tell her
Junie was gone.

But before Eddie could get home with that news, Susan
was out on a horse looking for him. Strange, by the time he
met her on the trail, he wasn't sobbing anymore. He said to
her, "Well, how nice of you to come home for a change."

Susan, she just grinned in that way of hers with her head cocked on one side. "Oh daddy," she said, "how could you round up the calves without me?"

Then he remembered: sure there were calves. And Susan was his cowgirl; she liked the animals better than either of the boys or her mother. Well, Eddie gave a whoop, and he vaulted up into the saddle behind Susan. Now, suddenly, she'd shrunk down in size until she was a little girl, jogging ahead of him on Marvin's neck. Yes, it was Marvin indeed, two horses before Lester. Susan was jogging there and giggling when Eddie'd rope a calf. Susan would pull the rope in. Then the calf would disappear, and Eddie'd rope her another one. Finally, she was taking her little hands and rubbing them over his face. But Eddie . . . holy Christ! Eddie now had his hands around on Susan's body, all over her body, and she wasn't no little child again. She was sort of melting away under his hands, and now he was crying for her . . .

Eddie gave a snort and a groan and pushed himself up. His head struck a log; he was blind, didn't know where he was at except it smelled of wet pine. And, when he rubbed his face with his hands, his face was wet.

Slowly, he pushed up out of the lean-to; remembering now where he was, the longhair and that girl. A few yards beyond, he could hear Lester chomping. Eddie moved over toward the horse, fumbled out a cigarette, and lit it. Then, still shaky from the dream, he leaned his head against Lester's withers and blew the smoke into the old horse's wet shoulder. It seemed in that moment that he could see those dead bears so clear; and indeed one time he had cleaned up a den like that. A hunter had stumbled onto a sow one spring, shot her as she went into the hole and asked Eddie to get his trophy out for him. But the damn lieutenant from Okinawa wasn't in the true story, nor was Junie, but Eddie guessed that most everything now had to do with Junie being taken away. And then—here in the dream for the first time—must have been Susan being taken away from him, too. He could feel her, he could smell her when she was a little thing and used to put her mother's perfume in her hair. And he could remember her lying in the bed with Doll and him when she was so tiny. But now, Susan's body in his hands? Eddie swallowed hard and scrunched his eyes shut as if to squeeze the thought of it away.

That was when he heard the girl say: "Is it easier sleeping standing up?"

"Huh?" Eddie pulled back from Lester. "Well, by God, it might be."

"You were—sort of thrashing around. Did you have a nightmare?"

"I guess."

Then the girl moved closer to Eddie and gently rubbed Lester's nose. Her slicker was open in the front, and her black sweater protruded through it. Her voice was a little husky and curious-sounding. "What were you doing out here? I mean tonight, when we found you?"

"Well," Eddie said, "it'd be hard for you to understand, but I wasn't chousing you birds and bees people. No, there's a big moose out here, hell he's a trophy. I was running him back into this godawful timber so the Game and Fish bastards can never get him."

"So you can kill him yourself?" the girl said.

"Mebbe someday. Not now."

In the darkness Eddie could see her teeth as she laughed in that husky little way. "You're a funny man," she said. "I've never met anybody quite like you." Then she turned and went back over to the lean-to. By the time Eddie'd finished his cigarette and gone over to the hutch himself, the Benny one was also awake and appeared to have been arguing with the girl; she kind of humped on her side away from him and pulled the poncho up over her shoulders. Eddie also saw that the Benny one, that hairy bugger, had changed positions so that now he was sleeping next to Eddie where the girl had once been.

Eddie chuckled a little as he hunkered down, and this time he didn't dream any more.

CHAPTER 7

THE house Susan Bulwer and the other stewardesses lived in was twenty minutes from L.A. International Airport. In fact, as Doll and Susan lay out on the beach together, they could see the planes, like silver wasps, whining off the runway and climbing out over the Pacific. "I hope it's going to be a nice rest for you, Mamma," Susan said.

And, Doll had to admit, the first few days of putting her old bones into a bathing suit and lying out in the hot sand made her believe she must have been in heaven. Susan and her roomates were awfully cute to Doll. That second morning one of the girls had made a special trip up to Malibu and bought Doll a new bathing suit. They'd done wonders with these things lately, Doll reflected; they tucked in and puffed out at just the right places, and Doll, in the mirror, even caught herself sneaking glances at her "figure"—Lord, she thought, it had been a long time since she'd used that word!

Speaking of figures, the roommates and Susan all looked like movie actresses. Doll noticed that Susan had learned how to paint her eyes and swirl up her hair; she'd even taken to dying it so there were little blonde streaks in the brown. And Susan had always liked dancing, but now the record player was going constantly; Susan would be twitching around out on the slat porch overlooking the sand; one of the other girls played a guitar, and she'd strum and sing. The third girl—Doll couldn't quite believe this—she was black. A very sweet girl. Doll had hardly ever been exposed to blacks, and she found herself just staring at the poor girl, sometimes in real embarrassment when the girl's eyes caught hers.

But soon the novelty of California life seemed to be wearing off. Susan had to take a flight to New York, and Doll was alone for three days. Well, you could hardly call it alone. The other girls were there, sometimes entertaining their menfolk in whispers down in the living room of the beach house. After which the girls would sleep most of the day or lie out on the beach like limp cats. Mum's the word, Doll thought. They were not her children to raise. But what did bother Doll and then got to frightening her was that beach, the whole world she'd come into. Sometimes lying in the sand she'd look back up at the houses: they resembled orange crates, sitting on stilts, their walls driftwood grey as if they'd been soaked in the ocean for years; and others were cracked fading stucco or concrete dumps that looked like they'd once been part of piers or fortresses. It was all decayed somehow, these shacks sagging and unsanitary, with the sewers backing up and mingling with the tidal streams from the ocean. And the people just made Doll shudder. Along this beach were—Susan would smile—"swingers." Well, they ought to be swinging by their necks, Doll thought.

With the exception of a few old derelicts with peroxided hair who looked like either weight lifters or manicurists, the neighbors were mostly young and had absolutely no shame. They'd lie on the beach, fondling each other in broad daylight; at night, they'd strut around practically naked behind their picture windows, or they'd be lying out beside barbecue coals, smoking marijuana; and if not this, then somebody along the swingers' strip would decide on a party; in would come dozens of little sports cars, jamming the tiny street. Then, about sundown, a rock-type band would begin, blasting out its discordant nerve-jangling sounds far into the night. Doll would slide the glass beach doors shut and try to sit inside with the TV blaring, to drown it out, but Susan's house, like all of them, seemed to be built of tarpaper and matchsticks. You could punch your fist through the walls, and Doll felt like doing it one night when she could hear the foul-mouthed neighbors fighting, then making up noisily in bed.

When the sun would come again in the morning and Doll would lie on the hot sand, she'd forget momentarily how bad the nights were. But soon, even over the splash and suck of the waves, she could hear the first commuter traffic roaring down the coast highway. Then there'd be planes overhead and speedboats whining like gnats offshore. Restless, Doll would get up and go for a walk, wade into the soft green breakers. The water looked so refreshing. But once in it, splashing it on her face, Doll smelled oil and sewage; her feet felt sticky; they were covered with tar. Walking on down the beach, she'd pass a sign that would say Absolutely No Dogs. But there'd be packs of dogs ahead, some out with their masters and others just roaming loose. And all of them were ragging after bones and garbage and dead things, and dirtying the sand with their manure.

By then, Doll would look up toward the bluffs above the ocean where the fine houses and pink and yellow hotels sat. Beyond this, in her mind's eye, she could see the vast L.A. basin and, rising up from it, the burned-brownish cap of smog. Susan had said you couldn't smell it out by the ocean. But Doll sure smelled something a few mornings. And then, as she walked alone down that beach, there'd be an evil old man in a terrycloth beach robe who'd sidle up to her; or invariably there were two swarthy men who'd snicker and whisper to each other every time she passed. She'd look at the shack houses on their stilts, see the dark windows, and imagine more people peering out. She always wondered if any of these creeps came after her, who would hear her scream.

By the time Susan came home, Doll was scared and sad, too. She and Susan sat out on the porch alone that next morning, and Doll told her what she'd been hoping: that eventually she could persuade Eddie to come over here and settle down; get rid of the ranch, just go back to Beaver for a few weeks vacation in late summer or fall. But even Susan laughed at that one. "Oh Mamma, can't you see Pop here? He'd plumb croak."

Then Susan stretched her long brown legs and began rubbing sun cream on them. It seemed incongruous to Doll, Susan using her daddy's language, "plumb croak," and yet Susan here with her cosmetics and her jets and her swingers. Brave new world. Doll looked over at her daughter and said, "Honey, I don't want you living this life forever, not in this place."

"Who said I was?"

"Oh, you take to it all right."

Susan lay back on the beach chair, one of her arms flopped down at her side. "It was a very tiring trip, Mother. Now let's not have a thing about where I live. I was hoping you'd enjoy yourself here."

"I am," Doll said. "Of course. I just meant you haven't been raised like this, Susan."

"That's sure right. I was raised in Beaver, W-Y-O."

"And there are worse places!"

"Look, Mamma, dammit, I just wanted to do something I've never done. Did it occur to you that maybe you wanted to do that too, and maybe Pop did. But you never got out?"

"Doing what you've never done can get you in trouble, young lady," Doll said. "Just remember that and let's forget it."

"All right, we will forget it." Susan leaned back in her sunchair and closed her eyes.

Doll watched her daughter's face. The pretty little mouth twitched, the chin trembled. Doll wanted to go over to her and hug her, but Susan was too old for that now. Or they'd both burst out into tears, and what good would that do?

Finally Doll said, "Well, honey, I'm going in and call your father. I might catch him home around noontime. Like to see how he's holding out."

Susan said that'd be a good idea; she'd like to talk to Pop, too. In fact, she put in the call. As she sat in the sun picking at her long toes and smiling, the phone crooked against her shoulder, she did look so much like Eddie. A pretty Eddie, the scrunchy face and straight features, skin soft and freckly brown. And Susan laughed so much in the minutes she was on with her father, Doll was anxious and a little annoyed. Doll would say, "Honey, that's enough. You're running up an awful bill." Finally, Susan did give Doll the phone, and, by then, everybody was pretty well talked out. Eddie just said, Yas, he was keeping well; hadn't been no more word on the moose, and Susan would tell Doll all the news, which wasn't much.

Eddie never did ask when Doll was coming home, which was strange. It was only later that Susan got to mentioning the two city kids Pop had found. Some of the same outfit that had beat him up, and now he had 'em there in the house like a couple of jailbirds.

"Well," Doll said, "I hope he gets rid of that trash."

"Nothing of the kind," Susan smiled. "It's pretty smart of old Pop. He needed a cook for next week's hunters, and he wants you to have a nice vacation. So he's got the girl cooking and her boyfriend washing dishes. Can you imagine Pop with a pair like that? I just wonder what kind of freaks they are!"

"I wonder too," Doll said quietly.

CHAPTER 8

BENNY Seipp's father was a brain surgeon in Philadelphia. Benny himself was a senior at Hofstra, not knowing what he was going to do when he graduated, certainly anything but medicine. Benny had met Vicky Yeomans when Vicky was down from Smith at the Georgetown Nuclear Freeze. They had slept together in the back of an old school bus—physically slept side by side, that is; and they marched the Georgetown streets with the mobs, wore Indian headbands and that sort of juvenile scam. Then the next year, Vicky quit Smith and ended up in Manhattan studying art. Eddie guessed that made it nice for Benny because Vicky had an aunt who was always in Palm Beach, Florida, and Vicky stayed in the aunt's apartment.

Vicky was an odd girl in some ways, but damn pretty and out of Benny's league. However, Benny had read a lot of psychology, and Vicky seemed to have all sorts of locked up problems dealing with sex and diet and world affairs; since Benny was a good talker and sounded smarter than he was, he became a sort of small-bore guru to a very mixed-up Miss Vicky Yeomans. Eddie gathered that Benny would have loved to have married Vicky, but she wasn't up for that. No, what it boiled down to was that Benny had the VW bug and the in-depth psych rap sessions that seemed to help Vicky out.

So Vicky just traveled with Benny that summer; she was a girl who needed motion and challenge, such as shaming Benny into climbing that damn stupid mountain. Hell, Benny was a talker, an intellectual, not a Tarzan. And that's what seemed to really bug him now, seeing where Vicky had ended him up.

It couldn't have been more than eight o'clock in the morning, but Eddie had Benny out working for a good two hours, pulling the barbed wire off an ancient fence. Before that, he'd put Benny to work on a pile of junk over by the log buildings. It looked like it had been there since the Civil War, all overgrown with weeds, rats, and stink. Eddie had said, "Straighten that, son, put the rottens and punkies in a pile and burn 'em, save out the scrap iron in another pile." When that was done, Benny was to yank all the old nails out of a stack of boards as high as Benny's head. "You save the old nails?" Benny had asked incredulously.

"Not only save 'em but expect you to hammer 'em straight if they come out crook'd."

Finally, Benny was to walk about a half mile through the swamp, prying off this vile old barbed wire, rolling it in a neat loop that weighed about a ton and if you lay it down wrong would explode like a rusty coiled spring, ripping Benny's clothes and skin with the barbs.

Standing out there in the tall yellow swamp grass, Benny felt about like blubbering. He was exhausted; his leg ached him where he'd hurt it on the mountain, probably was infected, and sometimes got throbbing in the dark cold cabin where he slept alone. Vicky had somehow graduated to sleeping in the main house. Eddie Bulwer had put her in the one decent bedroom, and he himself was sleeping on the parlor sofa. All very quaint and chivalrous, Benny sneered.

This was the real hassle for Benny: He just couldn't get through to Vicky anymore. He'd say to her after one of these Death March kind of days, "Who needs this?" And Vicky would say, "I do. And you might even learn something yourself." Then it would get nastier; Benny would say something about the old man and those boring stories he'd always tell at dinner. Finally Vicky would say, "Well he's paying us, isn't he? If you don't want to make a dollar, I at least do."

"Big deal," Benny would say. "Ten bucks a day between the two of us."

"With meals!"

"Well, I'm just about," Benny would threaten, "just about ready to get into the VW and head home. I'm late for school now anyway, hanging around out here with you."

"Don't let me keep you."

Then Benny would pull back. "You have such anger, don't you? What is this, more hanging onto your father? Is that what all this is about?"

"All what about?" she'd say coolly. But her lips would tighten.

Then Benny would take hold of her soft elbows and draw her to him. He could always get her coming his way on the psych talk. For a few minutes, then it'd get better. Soon though, the old man would be striding around the barn saying, "All right now, reckon it's time to bring them horses in . . . " And Vicky would go scampering after him.

So Benny was somewhat in limbo that morning, knowing he ought to get the hell home and yet: how did you cut loose from a Vicky Yeomans? Not easy. Even now as he was pulling the lousy wire off the posts, he could see Vicky with Eddie in the doorway of the barn. Vicky had her tight blue jeans on, and her long blonde hair lay soft over her shoulders. She was leaning next to the butt of a horse. Eddie was apparently showing her how to shoe a horse. That was really something Vicky needed to know, living in Greenwich, Connecticut!

But then, as Benny watched, he saw Eddie start up quickly, walk around the end of the log barn. Benny hadn't noticed it either, but two green, official-looking pickup trucks had driven into the ranch. Several men with red shirts and big cowboy hats got out. Benny assumed these were Game and Fish Department men. The way Eddie had talked about them, they were the next worst thing to city trash. Benny thought Eddie seemed to take delight in how he was out-smarting them, running off their pet moose. Anyhow, the men gathered there by the door of the barn. Benny could see Vicky being introduced to them, then Eddie squatted down beside the log barn and lit a cigarette. This was called "visiting time," Benny knew, and that was a damn good signal to get out of the swamp and take a rest himself.

Benny edged over to the barn. The first thing he saw was the look on Vicky's face, sort of hurt and incredulous, like she'd just seen a pet dog run over. She whispered to Benny: "They're after the moose."

There was a big hail-fellow-well-met type, dark wavy hair and expensive hunting clothes—he was standing above Eddie with his palm against the log barn, leaning on it like he was holding it up. Benny could see he was pretty much of an operator in that Rotary Club, backslapping way. He'd sneak a look occasionally at Vicky as if he'd like to have her in his hotel room for an hour or so. "Well, Mr. Bulwer," he was saying, "I certainly don't want to cause any hard feelings here. The governor seemed quite anxious for us to get this moose. It was our understanding . . . but." He smiled. "There are lots of other times and places to hunt, I suppose."

Eddie just squatted there looking down at his boot toes and dangling the cigarette out the corner of his mouth.

"We're not done yet," said one of the redshirts. He was a young, serious-looking game warden. "Eddie, I warned you. You can't keep us out of the basin. You might just as well cooperate."

"I told you my reasons earlier," Eddie grunted. "Open this place once, and everybody and his brother'll be in here."

"Come on, let's go," said the city hunter with obvious impatience.

The game warden pointed his finger at Eddie and said, "You're going to end up losing that moose and everything with it. I knew you were stubborn, but I didn't think you were stupid." Then he turned on his heel and walked back over to the truck.

Vicky's face was tight and mad. She looked from the men to Eddie. "How can they threaten you like that? This is your place and everything—"

Eddie just pushed up and shrugged. He stood leaning against the barn, watching the trucks pull away.

"Isn't there anything we can do?" Vicky said.

Eddie shook his head. "Not much. Pray that them buggers don't find him, I guess." Then, even though he was far from finishing shoeing the horses, he turned and walked slowly back over toward the dark porch of the log house. Vicky followed him with her eyes until Benny finally snapped his fingers in front of her to wake her up. She gave a little jump, and that was an opportunity for Benny to gather her into his arms. It was time, he said gently, that they started thinking about going back East, maybe leave like, in the morning?

Vicky murmured, "I don't want to go if we can possibly help him."

"Well what help could you be?" Benny asked quite honestly. Then he made the mistake of adding: how did she know anything about moose coming from Greenwich and Smith?

Well, Vicky erupted with that one. Her cheeks got red. She pulled away from him. He walked a few paces after her, trying to jolly her out of it, but she kept saying, "Just forget it, smartass."

That's how Benny was left, standing in a damn barnyard in western Wyoming, staring after his girl as she went into the house to solace an old man. It was something Benny hadn't quite come across in Psych. It was also something he wasn't going to stand around very long and watch.

"Unfortunately," said the game warden Roush, "we do have a few old-timers left like Bulwer. They're still living back in the 1880s. They figure the game belongs to them. God knows they poach it whenever they want to, and they act like they're doing you a favor even to guide you."

"Is he a good hunter?" asked Ras Conant.

Roush gripped and ungripped the wheel of the truck. "Yas," he said finally, "you'd have to say he is. If you don't mind doing everything the hard way. He'd walk twenty miles rather than buy a gallon of gas."

Ras Conant had the Forest Service map spread on his knees. "He's got a helluva territory here," he said. "Look at those contour lines. Very steep, heavy timber. It'll be like finding a gnat on a camel's ass."

"Don't worry," Roush said. "We've got ways of opening this place up."

The following night, Ras Conant lay exhausted in a tent about five miles into Eddie Bulwer's territory. And Conant had to admit that Joline Roush knew what he was talking about. "Here's to you boys," Conant said, and had a shot of bourbon before getting inside his sleeping bag. He meant it. He'd hunted in a lot of places, but rarely had he seen such efficient young men as those who worked for the Wyoming Game and Fish.

As they'd begun the hunt that morning, Joline Roush had divided the Bulwer Basin into five great squares. Joline and another warden hunted with Conant, while a second team paralleled their course, usually riding another ridgeline and glassing all the country they could. Both teams communicated by walkie-talkie radio. In addition, while they were hunting the first square, Joline had assigned two youngsters in a jeep to cutting an access deeper into a remote area. They worked with chain saws, starting at the end of an old timber road and widening up toward a high lake Joline talked about. Joline pointed out to Ras Conant where, for instance, Eddie Bulwer had cut heavy timbers and lay them across the road so there'd be no access by car or truck. "You're not going to be very popular with him," Ras Conant said, as the Game and Fish crew cleared the trees away.

"It's National Forest," Roush said. "It's anyone's right to be in here. Besides, the ranger wants this trail improved."

By that first night, Conant and Roush's hunters had pretty

well covered square one. They'd seen some deer, a few elk tracks, and one yearling female moose. The country in this square was relatively open, gentle sagebrush hills and aspen, so Roush felt confident that they hadn't missed the moose in it. Unless, of course, he ducked back in there after the hunters had left. "And," added Roush, "doesn't matter if he did. We'll pick him up tomorrow by air."

Ras Conant frowned. "You're flying it? I thought that was illegal?"

"In the case of this bull, where we've got a difficult terrain, and you have a limited time, Mr. Conant, it's about all we can do."

"But is it illegal?"

Joline Roush nodded. "For the ordinary hunter, yes. Again, these are extenuating circumstances, Governor's Permit."

Ras Conant didn't like it. "If I get that trophy, and it's taken illegally, it won't be worth a damn, Roush. I'd just as soon have you call off the airplane business."

"I can't reach the pilot tonight. Unless you want me to ride out and drive to town. Why don't you watch how he works tomorrow, Mr. Conant, and then you can make up your mind."

Ras Conant got slowly into his sleeping bag. Frankly, he didn't know what to say about the plane. He'd used a Piper Cub on skis in the Arctic getting a record polar bear. And God knows you used Land Rovers everyplace in Africa. Perhaps, he thought, if the plane were just a spotter, not used in any way to herd the moose, as they did with the polar bear . . . he'd agree to it. But that was the good thing about hunting, Ras Conant thought. You went to bed so tired you didn't have long to agonize over any decisions. As he slipped off to sleep, he saw those five squares of timber, five days, and he bet with himself he'd get the moose on day and square four.

CHAPTER 9

"THEM sons-of-bitches," Eddie said. He had stopped the pickup with a jolt. At what had been the end of the logging road, there was now a swath cut through the timber. Eddie got out of the truck. He squatted down and felt a fresh cut sticky pine stump. A chain saw had done this. And the big dead trunks Eddie had laid over the trail were pulled aside. Eddie's boot scuffed in the dirt. Caterpillar tracks.

The girl Vicky had her jacket collar turned up against the morning cold. She stumbled after him. "Where are they going with this road?" she said.

"Just as goddam far as they please," Eddie murmured. "It'll be a highway for any of you—any of them backpacking dopeheads who want to get into the lake." Eddie kept shaking his head and murmuring: he never thought Joline would go through with it.

Then Eddie felt his face flush and his eyes burn. He walked slowly back to the truck. There was a rise up ahead, he told the girl. They'd follow the new road up that far and see what they could see.

Eddie put the truck into four wheel drive because the new trail they'd opened was still slippery with mud and deep in the matted leaves and wood debris of centuries. Seeing that swath cut through the dark timber pained Eddie as much as a scar on his own flesh. Here'd be a little trickle of a brook bulldozed out; then the blade would have cut through a nest of small blue spruce. Even the earth reddened here as the trail started to climb; it was like the ground bleeding too. The sidehill trail was steep, and, as Eddie bucked the truck

114

upwards, the darkness in the forest and the destruction got reminding him of Bougainville, then Guam. He told the girl that this was how the mopping up had gone on Guam. As the Japs fled deeper into the jungle, engineers and Seabees came in with cats and dozed out fire lanes. Overhead spotter aircraft circled lazily; then there were bigger planes with loudspeakers, hollering to the Japs that the island had been captured by the Americans, so any Japanese alive should surrender at once. They wouldn't be harmed.

"That's the difference," the girl said. "The moose can't surrender. He'll be killed anyway, and all this forest with him. For what?"

Eddie shook his head; then he gunned the pickup, and they came up the sidehill into a small park at the top of the rise. Here, the timber thinned and scaled off down a long slope, which had creeks in it and willows and elkweed in the bottom. The road seemed to come only this far. Eddie could see where the cat had chewed up the grass turning around. Then, too, there was a blackened place where a fire had been. "They must have camped here that first night," Eddie said.

The girl had already gotten out of the truck. She was pointing off toward the great silver gray cliff of the Spines. Silhouetted against the slide rock was a tiny red speck. Turning then, glinting in the pale sun, it came away from the massive range and out across the basin. Eddie could hear the whine of the engine. He knew the plane well, dodged it for years; it belonged to the Game and Fish.

"Can they do that?" the girl asked.

"They can do just about anything they want back here," Eddie murmured. "It ain't legal. If you and I got caught flying for that moose, they'd haul our ass to jail. But them fellers have permission of the governor . . ."

Eddie walked back to the truck and took out his field glasses. For several minutes he watched the plane hovering, then saw it drop low and begin circling a park in the timber.

Eddie was curious. He couldn't tell if maybe the pilot had spotted something. Wasn't any reason to circle like that if he hadn't. Suddenly Eddie ran around to the back of the pickup, got up into the bed, and then crawled up on the cab roof. From here, just barely with glasses, he could see across the dark lodgepole tops and into the park. He caught a glimpse of two red tents and several horses. "They're going in like a damned vacuum sweeper," he said, "taking every piece of the country."

"What's the pilot circling for?" the girl asked.

"They're camped in that park. I doubt he'd be trying to land there. But sometimes if he's having radio difficulty— I've seen it happen—he circles close above, and they can make contact. Reckon that's what they're doing. I was a little scared first that they'd located something."

Eddie got down from the truck cab and lit a cigarette. A wind was beginning to blow, and it struck the girl and him as they stood on the rise. He'd let her wear an old red jacket of Junie's and a hunting cap pulled down over her ears. Now, in the wind, her blonde hair streamed out and caught the sun like golden aspen shivering in the fall. The girl sucked air into her lungs and kind of stretched. She said what a beautiful time of year it was if you didn't have to worry about killing and this mess that was going on here. Then she asked if Eddie would mind if she took a walk?

Eddie said, No. There wasn't anything to do up there, he guessed. He didn't even know why he'd come, other than to see how those Game and Fish fellows were hurting him. Maybe Eddie'd take a walk with her; there were some little beaver ponds below, kind of a pretty place. He might do some trapping in them next spring. Then it struck Eddie too, almost with a sense of guilt, how the girl smiled when he'd said he'd walk with her. There was a lot in her like Susan, excitement, great strong feelings for things. And the guilt was that Eddie had left Benny back at the ranch pretty much on purpose; well, in justification, the kid did about one hour's work for the eight he was being paid, and Eddie needed that old rusted fence pulled down before some colt would get caught in it in the deep snow. Frankly, Eddie didn't care for Benny anyhow; he reminded Eddie too much of the other trashy buggers who'd beaten him up. In fact, Eddie never could understand why a girl as pretty as this Vicky could have hung out with that hairy bugger in the first place.

All this crossed Eddie's mind as he nodded and said, Yas, they'd stroll on down aways, see some of the forest. But Eddie hadn't but got to the edge of the timber when he knew something was wrong.

Idly, he'd been following the plane with his eyes. It had stopped circling now. That's what bothered him. If the plane had been in contact with the camp by radio, did it just now get a message? "Look there at the way he flew," Eddie said aloud. "He's gone direct to the blowdown, on the side of the mountain."

Eddie turned, ran back to the truck and got the glasses again. Up close, there wasn't any mistake. The pilot was now flying strips across the blowdown and working his way slowly up the densely timbered slope lying below the Spines. "Do you recognize that place?" Eddie asked the girl.

She shook her head.

"It's where I found you two. And where I run that moose into. Seems like suddenly they have got interested in it."

"But nobody except you and me—and Benny knew . . . "

Eddie's eyes met hers. "I wonder if they could have talked to that kid? He's back at the ranch. They could have come in there, got asking him questions."

She frowned. "Oh, I don't think Benny would dare tell them anything. I mean, he's not happy out here and gets in these sulks, but he wouldn't squeal . . . "

"I can't tolerate watching this much longer," Eddie said, glancing again at the plane. "They'll find that moose now, if he's still there. We'd best go on home."

It was nearly noon when they pulled up to the ranch house. Usually Benny was setting out on the porch having a beer this time of day; or, with Eddie gone, the chances were he was asleep. Eddie said he'd go over to the bunkhouse and holler him up while Vicky would wallop together a little dinner. But the bunkhouse was empty, the door rattling in the wind. When Eddie got back over to the main house, Vicky was waiting for him in the parlor. "I don't understand this, or maybe I don't want to," she said and handed him a note.

Eddie read it. The note was signed by Al Clements, the district forest ranger. He said he'd stopped by to see Eddie about a new timber road back into the basin. Then there was a P.S. "Your guest wanted a ride to town. He's gone with me."

Vicky shook her head. "I can't believe Benny would just up and leave. I—well, he's got the car and everything . . . "

"Where is his car?" Eddie asked.

"At a gas station getting repairs."

"Which one?"

She frowned. "Well, a green place . . . "

"Conoco?"

"Yes."

Eddie walked through the shadowy log parlor and went to the phone. In five minutes he'd found out all he had to know. The bearded kid had come in there; forest ranger dumped him off. He picked up his Volks and started down the highway toward the Interstate. "Damn," Eddie muttered after he'd hung up. "Didn't even wait to pick up his money. He sure must have hated it here."

"He hated me being here," the girl murmured. "I had something else to think about besides him." Then she bit her lip and sat on the arm of the old stuffed chair. "Dammit, I was counting on a ride east. I don't have any way to go."

"Well, if you're short of money," Eddie said.

"It's not the money. It never is . . . " Then she sighed

deeply, and her shoulders sagged. "Well, maybe it's a load off my chest, I don't know. And I suppose if he really wanted to hurt me, he could have said something about that moose. Or it might just have come out in conversation. He wouldn't think it would matter to the forest ranger, who's not with those other men."

"Them buggers are all together though," Eddie said. "And that's just about likely what did happen. Clements asking him how we run onto one another; the kid mentioned the moose, and then Clements puts it all together because he and Joline are working to cut that timber road in. No, by God," Eddie grunted, stalking out into the kitchen, "they have about surrounded me now!"

"But when we saw the plane go back over that mountainside, how could there have been time to tell what Benny said? He must have just left here around ten this morning?"

"The ranger's got a radio," Eddie answered. "They're always jabbering back and forth, Game and Fish and them." Then he walked to the screen door, stood with his hands in his pockets, and stared outside. "We ain't never gonna be certain what did happen," he said finally. "But the way they're going after that moose on that sidehill—whether they know he's there or just think he is—they'll end up with him. And beat me too, that's what it comes down to."

"You're not thinking of giving in?" The girl came around by the screen door, and a beam of sun lay flecks of gray in her eyes.

"Yas, I am. The way they're cutting roads, flying it, doing any goddamn thing they please, they're slowly taking me apart, and with it my permit too. Ah hell," Eddie grunted, "don't help to cry about it. You might as well get out some grub." He began rolling up his sleeves to wash. "Pardon me for going first, if you want to clean up."

"Oh Eddie—" She caught him by the arm, turned him to her.

For just an instant, Eddie had a feeling that she was Susan.

He could close his eyes and hug his little girl again. But where that would bring him was only into the past, the way things once were before the world started jamming in. Even this girl Vicky, she was crowding him, making him feel old, first wanting to pet her atop the head; and then daring him to be young too; take one step across that line, reach out for her pink soft skin. And lie in his bed alone at night, mourning that his youth had gone.

"I'll . . . put some soup on," the girl said and went quietly over to the stove.

After dinner, Eddie lay in the swing on the porch, hoping to snooze. He was still trying to decide what he should do. Then he sat up and had a smoke. Vicky came out, drying her hands on a towel. She seemed happier now. "I've got a terrific idea," she said. "I mean, I don't know anything about moose or hunting. My father does a little, but not like this. Anyway, if all this depends on your taking the hunter, why don't you take him and *not* find him the moose. Isn't that pretty smart?"

Eddie chuckled. "Honey," he said, "you been covering the same brain territory as me, I guess. I did look at that possibility. But I couldn't put it over on Joline Roush, and probably not on this hunter either. He's pretty savvy, from what they tell me."

"So then you've just got to lead him to the moose?"

Eddie nodded. "Looks that way." He rubbed out his cigarette against the porch railing, then picked up his old gray hat, and settled it on his head. "You hired on to cook for this next bunch," he said, "them that's coming next week. But now that your partner's gone, you can go too and follow him. Or you can come up and help feed the royalty."

The girl hesitated. "You know, for a minute, when Benny left, I did want to go. But not now. You couldn't run me out now. I can't believe there isn't some way to solve this—"

"I'll saddle up the horses," Eddie said. "You whack some grub and utensils together from that list Doll keeps in the cupboard above the stove. And bring plenty of warms, blankets, tarps. I got a feeling it's going to storm."

Eddie didn't know why he said that. And yet as he walked down the worn path toward the log corrals, there was a gray bleakness in the afternoon, and heavy fists of clouds were gathering over the Shoshone Range. But Eddie had anticipated this in the rising wind that morning; maybe the real storm he feared was the one building within him. For now he had that half-sick feeling of knowing he was beaten; and when a man gave up on his principles, he found he didn't have an awful lot left. Well, Eddie had done this. And hadn't even been smart enough to do it right at the start. No, he had to bull for a few days, fight 'em head on, and then quit before the end. Doll had warned him. Doll had even tried to persuade him that their life was all through here. And now Eddie felt even a deeper uncertainty. He wasn't listening to Doll. He hadn't once wondered what she would have had him do. No, he just got to talking it out with the young girl, listening to her instead, sending her into Doll's cupboards.

"Aw Christ," Eddie said and kicked open the barn door. He felt as powerless and low as he ever had in his life. But then, handling the horses, saddling up . . . maybe it was the familiar coming back, or just the dumb brute labor of his life: anyhow, it began to ease his mind and comb the cares away. He'd done all he could. It was in God's hands now: kill a moose and save what Eddie had left, if that was what was wrote in the Book. Eddie clumped onto the porch and took his 357 Magnum down from the rack. Put two boxes of shells in his jacket. The girl came out and watched him silently as he slid the rifle into the hard, cold saddle scabbard. Then Eddie gave her a leg up onto an old roan they called Briney, and they started back into the basin.

Vicky Yeomans cooked a meal like she'd never cooked in her life. On a grill over hot aspen coals, she broiled venison steaks, fried eggs, toasted bread; she threw some lettuce together with canned peaches, then spread out chocolate bars and cookies she'd found deep in the bottom of one of Eddie's panniers. As Ras Conant blew into his hot mug of coffee, his eyes twinkled at Vicky, and he said, "Say, tell me the truth. Does the governor have you on his payroll?"

"I hope not," Vicky answered, knowing a little bit about the governor from what Eddie had said. Then she began fumbling with the hot water dishpan, conscious of the eyes of all the men.

"Seriously," Conant continued, "you're a helluva camp cook. How long have you been at it?"

"Tonight."

Joline Roush winked at Conant. "We better wait till breakfast and see if her luck holds out."

"Now come on," Conant said. "I can't believe you've never done this."

"I haven't," Vicky answered. She wondered what they'd think if she told it like it really was: that her family had had a Guatemalan cook for years; even at Aunt Ruth's, in New York, there was a Puerto Rican couple in constant attendance. Vicky had hardly been in a kitchen in her life; her father would consider it an affront if any of the children ever had to lift a finger, waste precious time that could be spent in the arts or improving the state of the world. So Vicky's older brother had gone on into the Peace Corps and supervised cooking adobe bricks in Chile. And Vicky had spent a boring six months as a Vista worker in Oklahoma before returning to art school in New York. Vicky's father, Sherman Yeomans, was a graceful, cultured liberal who prided himself on knowing how to live. He'd left CBS to go to Washington during the Kennedy years. His specialty had originally been television news, but, when he'd gotten frayed by the rat race of it, he'd moved over to an advertising agency. In fact, he was vice president of the agency and was considered, Vicky knew, a big man in the business. It also hadn't hurt that Vicky's mother was a deVries, one of the pioneer Long

Island families. Helen and Sherman Yeomans lived what would be considered from the outside a fascinating life. They knew the beautiful people; they were leaders of thought and taste. And the only subject Sherman could talk to his daughter about was how her car was running. That was a Porsche she'd never cared one damn about and finally wrecked before she came west.

For just a moment in the smoke of the fire, Vicky's eyes stung; she could see the dining room in Greenwich or some cocktail party at the New York apartment; her father, gray, silver impeccable: untouchable. She, his daughter, was a pretty little thing to charm some particular guest. She hated what she saw, looking back; and, yet, loved it too, yearned for him, Sherman Yeomans, to be as proud of her as these men at the fire seemed to be.

Slowly, then, she looked at Eddie. The warden, Roush, and the others had been quite stunned when she and Eddie first showed up. Eddie'd grunted, yas, he reckoned now he'd guide 'em. Changed his mind. Then dourly he busied himself about the camp. Vicky could see how hard it was for him; his face would be dark and tight as he'd pull off the pack saddles and get the horses string-picketed for the night. Even during dinner, when he was usually loquacious with his old stories . . . tonight he ate hunched up next to a tree, back in the shadows. But now, finally, the hunter, Conant, had walked over to where Eddie sat and offered him a cigar. Lit it for him, then asked, as long as Eddie was now the boss, what would be order of march on the hunt in the morning?

It seemed to take Eddie a long time to answer. He walked slowly over to the fire, squatted down, and looked from Joline Roush to the young faces of the other game wardens and, finally, to Conant. "If you're hunting with me, mister," he said, "you're gonna earn that moose."

Roush's head snapped up. "We got in our licks today, some damn hard ones!"

"You're talking about the plane, I assume?" Conant said to Eddie.

"Yas I am. And the goddamn radios and the trucks and chain saws. That ain't hunting."

Conant nodded. "I couldn't agree with you more. I'm ready to do it your way, even if we miss on the moose."

"Well, that's about what's behind this," Joline Roush muttered. "Eddie figures if he can make it complicated enough, tire you out, you won't end up with that trophy, Mr. Conant."

"That's a goddamn lie!" Eddie said.

"Who are you talking to?"

"You!"

Both men were up now, Joline Roush, big-shouldered, powerful; Eddie, lean and bent-dried like an old piece of leather. For just an instant it looked like Joline was going to swing on Eddie; but then his hand dropped to his belt, and maybe that seemed to make him conscious of his uniform, revolver, or badge; whatever, his fingers opened stiff and he muttered, "I never will understand people like you. It's got to be all your way, so you can poach any game you want, keep the public out of it. Do it just like grandpa did. When are you going to wake up and realize those days are long gone!"

In the firelight, Eddie's face seemed to smoulder. As Vicky watched, his lips moved as if he'd answer Joline, but then he only stared at the fire. Finally, he pushed up his old greasy hat and took it off. Then he leaned over the fire and poked his cigar into the coals. He said quietly, "I reckon you're right, Joline. You been to college; you know how to manage game, you and them professors the Forest sends out here. So hell, it don't matter to them guys if you kill this moose with radio, plane, or a goddamn rocket ship, for all they care. But I do care, mister." Eddie nodded slowly and the cigar glowed in his lips; then his face went dark. "Because you're killing a lot more than this bull. You're killing this ground. This wilderness. You're killing the whole idea that there are still places a man can go to be free. Maybe I'm luckier than most, but that's what this basin means to me; and I only come to it because my pappa bled and sweated for it. But you will kill this too like the rest . . . "

"I got a job to do, Eddie," Joline said. "That's to bring the most use of the state's game and fish to the most people."

"Yas, you all got jobs," Eddie grunted. "Sure. The governor, he's got a job to sell off this moose to the high bidder here, man who'll do the state some good. And the good'll be another dam on some river; and some factory setting out there in the sagebrush using the water; and you look at the sky and smell the soot and grit; it'll streak for a hundred miles and lay on the leaves. But it's all for the good of the state. Just like, well, livestock is fine for the state, too, and tractors and land taxes. That's jobs. So you game managers put out poison baits to protect the sheep from coyotes. The first thing eats it is a badger. Hell, that's all right; nobody likes him. And when he's dead, coyote eats him and dies; then comes the black bear, eats the coyote. I have seen this myself many times back here. Bear is dead too; and the eagles and birds feed on him and they die. So you might kill four or five different species with one bait.

"But it's for the good of the people of Wyoming. And it's making jobs. So is the timbering, when they cut away a whole side hill like up here on Antelope Meadows or Jackdaw Pass. It don't hurt, they say, to clear-cut swatches through these forests, tromp down into the streams with bulldozers until they're so mashed in you'd never believe there was a stream there, and you couldn't get a goddamn minnow to live in it. No, it don't matter. And once you cut the forest apart for timbering, you got your roads in there; then comes your jeeps and your trailbikes, snow-machine pests in winter, and the game runs higher and higher until there ain't no more mountain to climb.

"Sometimes I get a dream that in a few years there'll be bones on the tops of all those bally peaks, way above timberline, where the game has all finally ended up, starved. And down below at the edge of the forest, like in here, along the streams, there'll be them goddamn shacks and tin trailers and outdoor toilets and bulging over garbage cans. Yas, Joline, you are right. My days are pretty well gone. Doll's been telling me that for years now. But what you're forgetting is that as long as I hold title to my ground, there ain't a man gonna come in and cut one blade of grass or soil it with one stinking strychnine ball. And if I stay on this permit, this Forest ground, the same will be true back here; if they don't know how to keep it from being cut and torn and people-tromped, then by God I will. I'll hold this sonofabitch until somebody among you college boys or politicians wakes up that there ain't no more left like this. That instead of killing more game each year, to build up your own jobs, you got to save more because if you don't brother, your big game animals are going to be curios in museums. And with 'em the big old fish and the forests and even the sagebrush flats. They'll find a way to kill them too, probably with their mines."

Eddie stopped abruptly, as if suddenly conscious of how long he had talked; that Joline was sitting scowling at the fire; but Ras Conant had risen; he was pacing slowly away from Eddie, hands on his hips. And he was nodding. Occasionally Vicky would hear him murmur, "Absolutely. How right you are."

But Eddie had stopped now, as if he'd said it all and had found no answer; that there was none. As one of the young wardens said to Ras Conant, "Sure, I agree with a lot that he says. But what do you do with the people? They're going to come. You can't stop 'em. They're going to come here by the hundreds of thousands until this place ends up one great big dirty park."

"Some of these legislators in western states," Ras Conant

murmured, "just don't know what they have. They'll sell it all for a buck. And the worst part is, I've got a need too. I've got to keep a payroll paid and happy. I'll buy. I'll bring my people in here . . . " He shook his head sadly and glanced out toward the tents. "Eddie, in the morning, what time do you want to start?"

"Well before daybreak. I'll get you up . . . "

Then Eddie's voice trailed away. He'd walked out around the back of the tents. Hurrying, stumbling in the dark, Vicky went after him, then called to locate him in the darkness among the pines. His answer seemed far off. "Horses been making a little racket down here. I'm going to check on 'em."

"Can I help you?" Vicky asked.

"No need . . . "

Still, she took a few steps toward him; but when she reached the edge of the wet meadow where Eddie had picketed the horses, she stopped. Her eyes were used to the light now. She could barely make out the dark lumps of the horses, hear their snorting and mysterious eating grunts. Somewhere among them Eddie moved, until she could no longer see him at the far edge where the meadow joined the timber.

She wondered why she'd wanted to run after him. Was it sympathy for him, the way his voice had tensed tight and his face gnarled with bitterness? But surely he knew that she agreed with what he'd said. So it wasn't just to tell him, to comfort him, that she'd wanted to follow him into the darkness. It was to cling to him, like gripping the mast of a sailboat on Long Island Sound. In a sense, Eddie seemed like a man in a masquerade, his funny way of talking, his countrified manners.

The others, Roush, Conant, the young wardens with their trucks and machines, on the surface they were the reality. And yet, strip away their uniforms, take them out of the timber, and put them back in Vicky's old world in the East, they would be no different than the other men there, including and mostly, her father. Somehow, the old earth wisdom, the animal instinct, the quiet reverie of loneliness was gone from these men. For they, like Vicky herself, had been lockstepped into the stamping mill of modern American life. Lost touch with the stars and the sea and the track of a deer. Gone to schools which were little miniatures of the system, taught not how fish spawned or how a tree grew, but only how to adjust to boredom, how to beat the system by doing just as little work as possible, and still get by.

But Eddie Bulwer had missed this. His life appeared to be a total commitment, to have honesty and freedom. Vicky felt a desperation to be free too. Maybe, she thought, that's what the night in the forest and the days with Eddie Bulwer had done: made her stop looking inward and feeling sorry for herself. Looking instead at sweat and moose droppings and chill and life and death; and feeling in the simplicity of it all, comfort and hope.

She watched in silence a few minutes more, but Eddie never came back across the meadow. For all she knew, maybe he slept out that night; or just sat on a log smoking and staring at the cold stars.

CHAPTER 10

AT breakfast, in the black chill dawn, Eddie made it clear he didn't want any of the boy wardens along; or the girl for that matter; just more people to talk, more branches to crunch. He'd tolerate Joline, because he guessed Joline would have to be there in some official capacity, and Joline said, Yeah, that was right. So Eddie, Joline, and Ras Conant left on three horses while it was still dark. One of the boy wardens ran after them and said, "What about lunch? Shall we meet you someplace?" Eddie answered he had sandwiches already made.

Frankly, Eddie had several good reasons for not wanting a crowd along. Noise and commotion never did go with hunting, and, the fewer people who learned the byways of Eddie's back country basin, the better he liked it. Then too, Eddie still wasn't sure just how much Joline Roush knew. That is, Joline had never said anything about the kid, Benny, and whether Eddie had crowded the big moose back up in the blowdowns. As they jogged along in the dawn mist, Eddie wondered if the kid had squealed? If he hadn't talked and the plane had just flown the slope by accident—or by Joline's instinct—then there was still a chance that they'd miss the moose, and finally the hunter would give up.

This remote possibility Eddie found quite pleasing, in fact, humorous. Here he was, guiding up a storm for Joline and the governor, and maybe, by God, the moose would give them the slip after all. So Eddie chuckled aloud and began directing Lester down a long slope of sparse aspen. The first sun had just slid out from under a cap of streaky clouds; the world smelled sweet and dry, and there was no sound but the creaking of leathers and the shuff of horses in the aspen leaves.

"Are we going to ride all the way?" Ras Conant asked, pulling abreast of Eddie.

"We better not be," Joline said suspiciously.

Eddie grinned. "Hell, Joline, we haven't gone a mile from camp yet. I wasn't expecting no moose right in here, was you?"

Joline grunted something about how most people felt moose had poor smell and sight; but by God he knew different, and he'd seen old bulls light out at the snap of a branch.

"There's a lot of ways they can beat you," Eddie said. "I have walked past 'em lying in the willows, not six feet away, and they don't move. I have also seen old bulls tippytoe out of a place you swear there's no gate to. But they are gone, and you never see 'em. And I have frankly been outrun by 'em too, particularly if you're in a swamp or a boggy place. There ain't no rhyme or reason, Joline, as to how we strike 'em. I have come in making more noise than a railway train and stumbled on the bastards; and I have been soft as a goddamn weasel and had 'em spook to the top of the mountain. Anyhow, we are just getting to where we can glass it, and then I'll decide how we go."

At the edge of the thin aspen timber, Eddie dismounted, and the others followed. A bluff broke off here quite sharply; it was an eroded place with some alkali soil showing through, and just beneath it was a bog that had sulphur springs in it. "This probably was a buffalo leap," Eddie said to Conant. "At least I have got skulls out of that bog below."

"Indians drove 'em in?"

"I expect. Then, whites, around the seventies and eighties."

"Shhh . . . ," Joline said sharply. He was lying prone at the edge of the timber and, swiveling on his elbows, was glassing the long crooked valley that lay below. Eddie, without even looking, had seen what Joline had shushed about. At least the glasses had pointed in that direction, and there was, out across the trickle of a creek, a black smear on the sidehill. A hundred times Eddie had swung to that and been sure it was a moose, but it never moved. It was a pretty smart combination of lichen on a rock and some dark willows shadowing it.

"Nothing there," Conant said. He had his glasses out too now and had focused on the same sidehill rock Joline had found.

"In the timber," Joline said, his voice tightening. "About two o'clock."

Eddie didn't need glasses for this one either. There was a purply stained place beside the aspen on the far side of the canyon; just inside the shadows of the trees, Eddie knew there was a spring, and, likely enough in the first sunlight, there'd be antelope or elk browsing here. Sure enough, he saw several rusty gold swatches of hair, partly hidden by the white aspen trunks; then something gray moving in the bog. About four elk and at least one deer. "Do you want any of them?" Eddie said. "Pretty good buck in there."

Joline half rolled over and grinned sarcastically. "They don't replace a moose, Eddie."

"Just thought I'd ask," Eddie said. Then he squatted beside Joline and Conant and lit a smoke. "This creek," he explained, "curves off there to the south, goes through a little canyon, then rises and heads in the big blowdown timber underneath the Spines. We can ride this creek bottom around . . . and we better had, because I've seen a lot of moose in here. But you're going to be doing some walking too and pulling your horses out of mudholes."

"Why not stay on the top and glass it as we go?" Joline said.

"Because you can't see into all the tangles and beaver

ponds. Just like I told you, that bull could be lying four feet from you in there."

"Let's go," Ras Conant said. "I'm not afraid to walk."

As Conant went ahead of them, Eddie heard Joline mutter, "I still think you could glass it."

It was a curious day, Eddie thought. About eleven in the morning, the sun seemed to burn through the clouds, burn hotter than hell for fall. And there they were in the damn stinking bottom, along the little creek. The place was honeycombed with badger holes and old beaver runs; a horse or a man could crash through the sod top and be stuck down four feet with his foot in water. There were little beaver ponds along the creek and wet swales and new beaver-cut timber that Eddie had forgot about. The men went in single file, leading their horses. Occasionally, as they'd break out of the willows onto a little black pond, there'd be a slap of wings and a spray, mallards and widgeon cackling up scared and the horses spooking in the suddenness of it.

Eddie was sweating by now; he'd pulled off his hunting jacket and tied it on the saddle. Conant had stripped down to a black-and-white check shirt; he wore a big African hunting hat with a scarlet rag tied around it, to comply with Wyoming big game regulations that you wear something red. Occasionally, Conant would take the hat off and mop the sides of his neck with the red scarf. But, observing him, Eddie liked the way the man moved. He seemed to know the exact places to be looking for a moose; they'd come up over a little rise in the streambed, see a swale of elkweed and willows beyond. Conant's eyes would snap and sweep that swatch of country. He always talked in a whisper, and not much at that, and his pant legs didn't screech together like many of the dudes Eddie took out.

After three hot hours on the creek, and seeing nothing more than ducks and one beaver, Eddie was about half sheepish. Maybe it hadn't been plumb honest of him to come along here, when the chances were the big moose was still back up in the blowdown. And yet, the creek pretty well fed out of the blowdown, and any respectable hunt would have to cover it. This was about what Eddie explained to Conant when they hunkered down at the edge of a beaver pond and ate a sandwich.

Conant was kneeling like a big overgrown kid, tossing crumbs of bread into the pond. In the slanting sun streaks penetrating the misty water, Eddie could see two large brook trout near the beaver dam. They were fanning a yellowish place in the mud bottom, like gold miners rustling little pebbles of color in their pan. Those brooks had wide green-backs, beautifully spotted fins, and, when the sun struck their sides, there'd be a shimmering of reds and whites.

"Look at that," Conant said. "They don't take the bread crumbs at all."

"They got their mind on other things," Eddie said. "Spawn-ers."

"Oh. Well by God, they're nice fish." Conant moved away from the edge of the dam, stretched, and lay back on the beaver-cut logs, hands under his head. "In fact," he said, "this whole damn place . . . unbelievable. Don't get me wrong. I like to shoot. I like ballistics. I find the kill exciting, even after all these years. But still, on a day like this, some-times I don't much care if I get the animal or not. You ever feel that way?"

At first Eddie was going to answer; but the words didn't quite form, so he just nodded. What he was going to say was: some days he didn't feel like leading a man to game either. No, it was enough to see and be out listening, working so hard and sweating, like along that bog, that your mind stopped tormenting with worries and fears, and when you finally ate you tasted every juice and when you slept you twitched into a deep peace. So sure, Eddie agreed with him. And it was a little sad too, Eddie reflected, because neither man could bring himself to say, *All right, we are enjoying*

*ourselves just walking, drinking in this world. Let's throw away
the guns. Let's quit killing for now.*

No, they didn't say that. Seemed to Eddie that he and
Conant both, and Roush, were all prisoners in their own
harness, like oxen pulling separate wagons. They just went
stomping along and couldn't shut off the twitch of the whip
that kept 'em going on and on. It was like life had become
roles, and if you were a bigshot game hunter, you had to
keep killing; and a guide, you kept leading. Like once Eddie
thought about a dam the state was going to build on the
Beaver River. Hell, not one person or any group Eddie knew
about wanted that dam. And yet, here she come clunking
along, the plans for it, the state engineer's people writing
new surveys and taking rock samples. It was just like the dam
was a great big caterpillar machine that had got rumbling
down a hill by itself, and nobody knew anymore how to reach
into the guts, jerk the wire, and shut her off.

So Eddie and Conant both got up from nooning by that
beautiful pond. Conant checked his rifle, and Joline stayed
close behind them leading the horses. Eddie had said that
the best part of this creek was where it came out of the
blowdown under the Spines. There was a meadow up against
the black timber, and moose grazed it often. In a pool there,
Eddie had found watercress, which was, he started to say, a
delicacy for moose.

He'd just put the words on his tongue when he felt Conant
stiffen beside him and drop into the sagebrush. A good four
hundred yards away, up against the edge of the timber
grazed three moose: a cow, a yearling, and the big bull.

Eddie had been walking just behind Conant when they
came over the sagebrush ridge; that's how Conant had seen
the game first. And in the surprise of it, and final discovery,
Eddie dropped to his knees and felt a little weak. Maybe he
hadn't had enough lunch; or it was the knowing that they'd
eventually have to find the bull, and some hunter beside

Eddie would be lying in the sagebrush, glassing him and breathing: "Jesus Christ, will you look at that head!"

By now Joline had wriggled up too. "I guess he shows we weren't exaggerating, Mr. Conant."

"He doesn't wind us; he doesn't see us," Conant said.

"Naw," Eddie murmured, "he's just standing there fat, dumb, and happy, eating watercress."

Eddie watched him in the glasses. The bull was kneeling now at the edge of the small pond, his rump in the air and his great black snout gorging into the water plants; then his rack would shiver up in a spray of water and weeds as he chomped and looked over at the cow and yearling. It seemed obvious they were waiting for their chance to eat too, but only when the king was done.

Eddie heard a rustling. Ras Conant had wriggled a few inches forward and was now in the prone position, thrusting aside a tall sagebrush with his rifle barrel to get a clear field of fire. "You ain't shooting from here?" Eddie whispered.

"I've got Magnums. I can reach him."

"Yas, but only cripple him, Conant. You'd never kill him from here."

Conant scowled. "Then I might as well say good-bye to him. Look at this: all open, we've got no possible way to sneak him."

"It's the hunter's choice now, Eddie," Joline said tightly.

"But it ain't," Eddie grunted. "I brought you this far, found you the goddamn thing, now you do it my way. He's too good to cripple and let wander off to die."

"Well, you're too late already," Conant said, "sit here talking about it—"

Then Conant raised up on one knee. And to Eddie it was like that old bull had heard him arguing to save his life. For no reason at all, it seemed, the bull had now gathered himself up, and Eddie saw just his black rump edging into the lodgepole timber. For a moment or two more, the cow and yearling took their turn at the watercress; then they moved up the trail after the bull.

"He couldn't possibly have heard us or winded us," Joline said. "What moved him? Do you suppose there's somebody else up here?"

"There could be, if you been talking about it all over town," Eddie muttered. But then he glanced up at the sky; there were clouds again over the sun, and the air had turned suddenly chill. "The wind has switched," Eddie said. "Weather coming." Then Eddie walked back and brought up the horses. "We'll go around the edge of the timber to pick up that trail he took. Then we go on foot."

"Hell, Eddie," Joline said, "why circle around the edge of the timber? It's twice as long. Ride straight across this sagebrush basin. We can see where he went in."

"If you want him," Eddie said quietly, "you best listen to me. He is probably standing in that timber edge watching us. You ride across, in plain view, you'll spook him good. And that's a bad enough place anyhow, that blowdown. It'll be all you can do to get him in there."

"Which would please you if we missed," Joline said.

"Come on, dammit," snapped Ras Conant. He spurred his horse off, circling left toward the protection of the timber. By the time they'd reached the trail the bull had entered, the wind had stopped, and there was a heavy cloud cover, faint pattering rain. "Take your slickers and food and whatever else you can think of," Eddie said. "We're likely to be doing some walking."

Eddie had never been exactly in this part of the blowdown. For perhaps a quarter mile, the forest floor was flat, dark with rotting trees; and there'd been a lightning burn here too. In the increasing rain, water was puddling at the bases of the giant trees. Climbing over the limbs and trunks, Eddie felt his trousers soaking through, and his hands grew cold enough to draw on gloves. By now, he'd lost the track of the big bull; it seemed like there were moose droppings everywhere but for trailing, there were simply too many scarred rotted wood chips, leaves, pine cones on the earth. We need snow, Eddie thought to himself; and maybe it would come before dark.

The visibility grew worse now, too. Finally Eddie separated himself from Conant and Joline, had them each take a beat about fifty feet from him. They proceeded across the great level blowdown in the direction of the Spines. A half dozen times Eddie would see a dark patch of hair; he'd stiffen and then come up only on the wrinkled side of a giant lodgepole. There was no game at all moving now as the rain increased.

Soon, the level forest floor played out. Ahead, Eddie could dimly see the first sharp rise that led up toward the Spines. There was a trickle of a spring here, coming out of a sharp canyon. Eddie whistled Conant over to him, said he thought this spring might lead up to a place where a moose would go.

By now, Conant was soaked; his eyes seemed sunken, and he looked tired. Joline, on the other hand, had a freshness about him as if he'd just figured it all out. "Now, this is up to Mr. Conant, of course," he said, "but my vote would be in this lousy rain to leave him set. This is a trap back here. That bull can't go anyplace. We camp at the edge of the timber, and we'll have him by morning, particularly if it snows."

"I don't intend to leave him," Conant said.

"Well, I'm trying to guarantee him for you, that's all. It's noisy now with these rain shirts; there's no visibility. I wouldn't want to run him out of here or have him double back on us."

Conant blew his nose, then wrung the water out of his African hat. "What do you think, Eddie?"

Finally, Eddie said, "Well, I don't want to get him at all, but I have told you I'd help you, so I will. We had best keep on him, starting with this here spring."

Now Joline really looked tired; and Conant was dragging

along, too, as Eddie started up the slippery hill where the spring trickled down; then it narrowed into a canyon that was brambles, thickets, mud, and rock that you'd slip and bang legs on. Eddie hadn't gone a hundred yards up before he heard Joline cussing it, then whispering loudly: "We're going up on the sidehill. You can see this whole bottom anyhow, don't have to plow through it." Then, pulling their way up by hanging onto branches and willows, they crawled up the steepest part of the sidehill and were soon lost from Eddie's view up in the timber on the crest.

He was alone then in the canyon. The rain was coming down so hard now a mist was boiling up off the little stream which had widened. Far distant up in the Spines, lightning crashed. What a day for a man to be out doing this, Eddie thought. Then, in the burned, wet smell of that canyon, and the distant crashing, it seemed again to Eddie that he was back in the war. He was out in front of some tomb on Okinawa; from inside, there were eyes watching him. He could almost smell it again, the burned flesh.

But then death was gone; even the sounds of the battle had died; the lightning silenced, and now the rain was freezing into a soft snow. Eddie was standing beside the trickle of spring and realized that the canyon had played out in a sheer cliff. Ahead of him, in yellow shivering willows, stood the massive moose, alone. He faced Eddie directly, his eyes black shiny, his teeth baring slowly; then biting with a loud snap and out of his nostrils a boiling steam. For the bull had looked behind him, long before Eddie had realized it, and he knew he was trapped. The sides were too steep to scale: the only way he could get out was to thunder back over Eddie. It only took an instant for the brute to know this. His black silver-tipped hair had stiffened over his massive withers; he was pawing blood-red cuts in the wet earth, snapping his teeth, grunting, and then he charged.

In this moment, Eddie's rifle went up automatically to his shoulder. The moose was thirty feet from him, leaping out of the willows to twenty, ten. And Eddie was saying, like Vicky the girl had said, "So you can kill him yourself?" And Eddie had answered. "Not now. Maybe sometime . . . "

There was a roar of a shot, a fist of sound slamming, and in that black avalanche of moose body, unstoppable, Eddie's rifle was flung away. Eddie felt black knobs slam into his shin, his hip, he was twisted down into the willows, his eyes pulsing with stars as he tried to gulp air and suck back to consciousness. Then, dripping wet, down on all fours like a dog in the willows, he realized he hadn't been knocked out at all. But he had been hit a helluva blow, his neck twisted, his leg and side aching. And just beyond him, going at a proud trot with that rack tossed back, the big bull soared away and plunged down the last hill in the streambed that Eddie had climbed. Then the crashing subsided, and he was gone. "For Christ's sake," Eddie murmured. "Did I miss him? I must have missed him."

But there was no smell of powder. Eddie crawled over to reach for his gun. Then above him, in the echoing timber, another slamming shot and a cry: "That's him, Joline. I have him now!"

Eddie scrambled up, unable at first to believe it. He jerked open the breech of his gun. Same shell. No. He hadn't fired. He was just ready to fire when the moose charged him. But there had been a shot. And now this shot. Eddie whirled and looked back down the streambed where the moose had gone, half dreading to see Joline or Conant come sliding down the sidehill. But the canyon was empty, misty smoky, swallowing up the bull.

"For Christ's sake," Eddie murmured. Then he realized he was chuckling and blubbering at the same time. He scrambled up out of the canyon, and by then they were shouting for him. Up top, on the ridge, maybe a quarter of a mile away, Ras Conant knelt stroking the neck hair of another giant bull moose. "They were up here, Eddie," Conant cried. "About five of 'em. Joline took me right into the center of 'em." Then Conant chuckled and wiped the water off his face. "Well, Eddie, what do you think?"

"That's a helluva moose," Eddie said.

Conant had a tape measure out now and was pulling the big horns around to get a spread on them. "I don't know enough about the Shiras moose record," he said, "but damn, he looks like he ought to be up there someplace."

For the first time now, Eddie noticed Joline. He was leaning against a lodgepole with his rifle slung barrel-down over his shoulder. Everything on Joline—his hat, his eyebrows, his gunsight—was dripping water. "He might be in the records," Joline said quietly. "But way down. He's a good moose all right. But he is not the moose. Not the bull we saw, or the one we glassed. I tried to tell you that before you shot."

Conant frowned. "I heard you. And hell, Roush, I think this has got to be that same head. Of course, you fellows have seen him more than I have, and closer. Eddie?"

Eddie happened to glance up, and his eyes met Joline's. The warden looked almost like he had his ticket book out to sign. "Are you going to say, Eddie?" Joline finally snapped.

"It ain't the moose, Conant. You shot a good one, you had a good hunt, but you got the wrong one." Eddie chuckled. "God bless you . . . "

"Did you see the other moose, Eddie?" Joline glowered.

"He went back down the hill. You boys should have followed me."

"Then we can still get him," Joline said. "Starting to snow now. We can pick him up before dark."

"I don't believe you can, mister. Now dammit, I lived up to my part of the bargain. I guided you fair. But when you start taking two moose on one permit—"

"The governor wants Conant to have that big bull. This one was a mistake."

"I mean it, if you try to shoot two up here, Joline—I ain't nobody in this state—but I will go to every goddamn newspaper, lawyer, and politician I can to hang that governor, and you with him—"

"Forget it, Eddie," Conant said quietly. "It's like you said. I did have a good hunt, a helluva hunt. Maybe I'll come back next year, and we'll take the big one, now that I've learned a little bit about how they work." He smiled and pushed up from the moose head. It was snowing harder now, dusting the hair on the animal's back. Eddie had never had a moment in his life when he loved moose so much.

Then, after they opened up the bull and gutted him, they started down the trail, their arms hot and sticky with blood. It was a beautiful dusk in the softly falling snow and the big timber. Eddie walked like he wasn't tired at all; Conant whistled a bit like a big overgrown kid. But Joline Roush never said a word all the way back to camp.

That night after supper when the trucks pulled away, Joline was driving the last jeep in the convoy. And before he left, he glanced at Eddie and said quietly, "I guess you figure you put it over on all of us. Well, you didn't, Eddie. You'll be sorry we didn't come out of here with that trophy."

Then the Game and Fish trucks and jeeps pulled away; they took their chain saws, their horses, tents, radios; and the carcass of the good bull they'd sent some of the boy wardens out to get. It rode in the back of one truck with its legs stiffened in the air. From that truck, Ras Conant, he leaned out the window and gave Eddie's forearm a shake and said thanks again. Hell, Eddie thought, he didn't have to say nothing. He'd already left Eddie an envelope with a fifty-dollar check in it; more than that, he'd left him the bull.

So Eddie stood in the faint snow and waved the red taillights away. Then he turned and went back over to the cook tent. The girl was still here, of course. He'd tried to get her to ride back with the trucks, but she wouldn't go.

The girl was kneeling by the cookstove, her hair in pigtails and sweat on her face from the heat of the fire.

"By God," Eddie said, "I'm going to have me a whiskey. Maybe I'll just get drunk as hell."

The girl smiled at him and said, "Maybe I will too."

CHAPTER 11

ONCE the first snow came that year, it never left. Day after day, it drifted down over the basin, froze the Spines into stiff icicle fingers. Strangely, there was little wind with the snow; it fell heavy and soft and made Eddie's kingdom still as a tomb.

All the people had gone now. Conant; then the hunting party Eddie had had the following week; and finally the girl, Vicky Yeomans. She left sobbing one day when Eddie put her on the bus in Beaver. There was probably people in town, some of them miserable buggers that had nothing more to do but bad mouth—some of them undoubtedly saw that little girl hug Eddie so hard. And they'd surely be buzzing on their phones that Eddie had a ladyfriend, lady hell, some hippy kind of hoor with long hair and tight jeans. Eddie knew all this when he risked taking Vicky to town and putting her on the bus. And after she'd gone, he sat in his pickup, and he brushed at his eyes, already missing her.

Crazy, he thought, gone plumb mad. A little while ago, if one of them trashy buggers had tried to camp on him, he would have had a fit. But he never thought he'd cry for a little city girl who seemed so far off and mixed up, and yet, had, in her way, loved him, and he her too. Not once, not even that last night in the snow at the camp, had he more than put a hand on her shoulder. She yearned him to, he knew that much; and yet, it seemed like finally she got over needing him, or talking with him about her own father, and how he never gave her a chance to do anything, paid no attention to her from his busy life. In the end, Vicky just sweated there in the cook tent, took lonely walks in the moon, and, finally, like Eddie himself, got to whispering at the horses.

When she was about to leave, she begged Eddie to let her help him: make people back in the cities realize how this beautiful wilderness was being chopped away. In fact, she said her father, being a big man in the advertising profession, could help. Well, Eddie thought, maybe if she and her pop got working on this together, doing something together, they might get on better and bring that girl happiness in her heart. So Eddie said, half lying, Well, over the winter he would try to write her pop a letter, explaining some of the threats to the wilderness and plumb stupidities of the Forest and them. She gave him her father's business address, and hers too; the last thing she cried out was, Write.

Hell, Eddie intended to write a letter or two every winter, but once the snow set in and there was horses to feed, wood to carve, and game to taxiderm—Eddie never picked up a pen. That would be Doll's work, if and when she ever came home.

It was strange, Eddie thought, that he hadn't heard from Doll. Of course, he'd been off hunting and, after the hunters left, gathering horses and out letting down fences so the ice wouldn't break them in winter. He would have been hard to reach, after the girl left, the house empty for hours at a time. Finally though, he did get puzzled, and he called Doll at Susan's place in California. No satisfaction there. Some snippy girl answered, it seemed that Doll and Susan had taken a short vacation in Mexico, and the roommate wasn't exactly sure when they were expected back. "They didn't leave no place I could reach 'em?" Eddie asked.

The girl said they might have, but the house was a mess because there had been a robbery in it, and they were just now getting straight.

Good lord, Eddie thought, I wish Doll would come home, Susan too.

But after another several days passed—now the California number didn't answer at all—Eddie got a new sour sort of idea: that Doll was staying away because of what she'd heard around Beaver: that Eddie was living with a young girl. Doll had a lot of friends in Beaver, old lantern-jawed biddies with kerosene tongues; and if they had gotten talking, say to Ly and Ly's wife down in Casper, passing that along to California—Eddie stopped suddenly, and it bothered him that he just thought about Ly, Doctor Lyman, so rarely. Ly was still his boy, and he was proud of him, even though they weren't what you'd call close friends.

So Eddie, that very evening he was sitting with a glass of whiskey, picked up the phone and called Ly. There was a lot of noise in the background; Ly was apparently watching a football game on the TV. And Ly said no, he hadn't had any word from Mom, except a card from Mexico; but it was just Tijuana, right across the border, so maybe they hadn't traveled far. "Don't worry, Pop," Ly said. "It does her good to get out. You might say this is the first real vacation she's had for years. It's just too bad she's not home with you now. I imagine you're pretty upset about it."

Eddie smiled. "I'm getting tired of my own goddamn cooking, that's for sure."

"I don't mean that," Ly said. Then his voice dropped. "Pop, didn't you see?"

"See what?"

"Why, the Casper paper yesterday. The Game and Fish Commission met. Had the usual news release about game seasons, numbers of kills for the year. And citations. They had you there, Pop, for that business this spring. They took your permit."

Long after Ly had hung up, Eddie just sat in the big chair by the fire, and, finally, when he had to throw something, he threw the damned empty whiskey bottle into the fire. By then he was swarmy drunk; he rubber-legged out into the snow, banged his head going into the dark shed to get out the pickup. It seemed like then he'd known for all his life they were going to lift his permit. It was just that the sons-of-bitches should have the decency to tell him like a man, not let him hear it from some commission printed in the newspaper. But then it did occur to Eddie that he hadn't been to Beaver for nearly a week to get his mail. And the chances were Joline wasn't exactly hankering to pick up the phone and tell Eddie the news.

So now Eddie was in the shed with the pickup started; and that gave him the idea of what he was doing in the truck: he was leaving for town, to pick up the letter in the mail, ending his life as a hunter. And then he would go to Joline and pound on that bastard until . . .

Until when? Eddie thought.

He had the truck backed out now. But slowly he reached up and shut off the engine. Running to get some damned letter and fighting to have revenge wouldn't help nothing now. It seemed to Eddie that he was tired out, worn out of fighting. He just somehow wanted to lie down and sleep; dream then about all the good times he'd had out in the mountains and the streams: times he'd never see again. Some new outfitter would be back in the basin now; new people coming in, backpackers and dopeheads camping at Grubbing Hoe, the Forest and them cutting roads. And Eddie sitting out above the Pacific at a parking lot, his arm around . . . Around who? Susan? Vicky? Doll?

Then his face got warm; his head was burning on one side. When his eyes finally opened, they stung like they had that morning at the old Morris Hotel. Because the sun was up and bright on the snow, glaring into Eddie's eyes off the hood of the pickup. And when he looked out, his eyes followed a slow familiar track up until he saw the old log barn with the horses standing outside in the deep snow, waiting to be fed. Turning, Eddie could see the gentle swale of the little creek in the meadow, loafed over heavy with snow. And closer, the buck fence around the house, the heavy pines; and a tire track. In front of the house was a strange auto, a dark green sedan a few years old. Eddie, sleepy, his eyes burning with whiskey smarts and chilled from sleeping in the cold truck cab—he came to slowly, knowing he recognized that car from someplace. Then he was turning to look out the other window of the pickup, and, all at once, he knew the car: it belonged to the clinic in Beaver. And who had driven it out, because she had no way to get home when she got off last night's bus—there was no answer when she called because Eddie was out here drunk, sleeping in the pickup. In the bright snow sun, staring at the pickup like Eddie was dead, stood Doll.

Her high cheekbones were glistening, tanned; she had a new hat on, kind of a fur Cossack outfit and a big muff to match. And she was talking to Eddie then, but he couldn't hear the words, the windows were still rolled up in the truck.

She ran toward him, half stumbling in the snow. Eddie burst out of that truck and seemed to leap a dozen yards to her, soaring into her like that great old bull who had gone free down the hill. With strength Eddie didn't know he had, he was swinging Doll up so just her boot tips brushed the snow; and hugging her narrow shoulders and soft breasts to him, and the perfume that could only be her drugged him as it wafted from the warmth of her neck. "Jesus Christ," Eddie whispered, "don't you never go away again."

She was shaking her head and sobbing, until Eddie said, holding her chin, "Damn, I thought you'd *moved* to California."

She did smile then, sniffling and rubbing the back of her hand over her nose. "We aren't moving anyplace, Eddie," she said. "Aw God I'm glad to be home."

"Well, it ain't much now," Eddie said. "It's just the ground here, Doll, not the basin anymore. They have taken the permit away, like you said they would."

She didn't appear to be listening. She was looking up at him and running her gloved fingers over his cheeks. "I'm the luckiest woman in the world," she said, "I knew it always and forgot it too. Did you really think I'd move out, take you to California?"

"Well, I fought and bucked and kicked at it. But without that permit, you may be right, Doll. Maybe we ought to move someplace, because we ain't got much left here."

"Eddie," she said. She gripped his hand now and began to lead him toward the car. "We've got it all here, if only we can see it and treasure it. That's what I saw, Eddie, out there in Susan's life, then stopping down and seeing Ly in that grubby little subdivision at the edge of town."

Eddie frowned. "He didn't say you'd been there."

"I asked him not to. I was just on my way to Cheyenne, didn't want to worry you."

"You went to Cheyenne?" Eddie said.

They had reached the car now. Smiling at Eddie, Doll nodded, then opened the car door. There on the front seat was her blue traveling bag and a stack of groceries and the mail Eddie had left so long in Beaver. But she didn't touch anything on the seat except her purse. Out of it, she drew a long envelope and without a word handed it to Eddie. On the corner was stamped Wyoming Game and Fish Commission. Slowly, Eddie drew out the single sheet of paper. The first name he saw was Mrs. Edward Bulwer typed across the center of the form. It was an Outfitting Permit for Mrs. Edward Bulwer.

Doll was standing there, his Hungarian girl, a trained nurse, mother of his kids—Doll who had never shot or fished in her life: she was standing looking up at him with her chin trembling and her eyes glistening with tears.

"Them bastards!" Eddie roared. "You did it to 'em, honey. You showed 'em another way, didn't you, by God! Taking out your own permit. If that don't beat it. I never thought of that, Doll." Then Eddie was hugging her, twirling her up like they were dancing in the snow.

"They didn't want to give it to me at first, Eddie. But I got like you, fighting mad, I got a lawyer and contacted our state senator. It's perfectly legal that I can hold the permit, and, furthermore," Doll was laughing, "I'm honest. They'll never catch me with too many fish, or hunters off killing elk out of season."

"No," Eddie said, "I reckon they won't catch you. The fact about it, good a hunter as I am—I was plumb lucky to catch you myself." Then he grabbed her around the waist and half lifted her again. "Well," he said, "you may have the permit, but I ain't your cook. Are you going to starve me or freeze me to death or what?"

"Love you to death," she said.

And so they stayed, and they're still there now: Eddie Bulwer's ground, a kingdom saved by his queen. But he knows that this wilderness will die when he does. For they're the last—Eddie's kind—the last to see the elephant of the pioneers, and the great bull moose that got away.

If you have enjoyed this book and would like to receive
details of other Walker Western titles,
please write to:

Western Editor
Walker and Company
720 Fifth Avenue
New York, NY 10019